A DEBT OWED

CLARISSA WILD

Copyright © 2019 Clarissa Wild
All rights reserved.
ISBN: 9781096519508

This is a work of fiction. Names, characters, places and incidents are either the product of the author's imagination or are used fictitiously. Any resemblance to actual events, places, organizations, or person, whether living or dead, is entirely coincidental.

All rights reserved. No part of this book may be reproduced, transmitted in any form or by any means, electronic or mechanical, including photocopying, recording, or by any information storage retrieval system. Doing so would break licensing and copyright laws.

PLAYLIST

"Hostage" by Billie Eilish
"Lovely" by Billie Eilish ft. Khalid
"Six Feet Under" by Billie Eilish
"Bury A Friend" by Billie Eilish
"Dinner & Diatribes" by Hozier
"Movement" by Hozier
"Power" by Isak Danielson
"Burn" by Cody Crump
"Hurts Too Good" by Ruelle
"Game of Survival" by Ruelle
"Daydream" by Ruelle
"Dangerous Woman" by Ariana Grande
"Skyfall" by Adele
"For The Damaged Coda" by Blonde Redhead
"Call Out My Name" by The Weeknd
"Handmade" by MARINA
"Style" by Taylor Swift
"Last Stand" by Kwabs

PROLOGUE

EASTON

A few weeks ago, age 25

I can't stop staring at the pretty pink-haired rich girl dancing in the picture on page five of the newspaper I'm reading.

"Davis heir celebrating a birthday while father's business on the verge of bankruptcy."

My lips curl into a vicious smile when I read that headline. Now this, *this* is something I can work with. This is how I'll get inside … how I'll destroy his multi-million-dollar business and get my hands on the girl.

Charlotte Davis; the daughter of my nemesis and my

lifelong obsession.

When we met for the first time at her father's wedding, I knew right then that she was made for me. It was never a choice, but she thinks it is. She thinks she can decide her destiny, but she's wrong.

I worked hard for years to build an empire for the sole purpose of destroying Davis Holding and taking Charlotte as my own. And I will get my fucking way.

The newspaper crumples in my hand as I get up and throw it away.

Time to make some calls and get to work.

ONE

Charlotte

Present, Age 23

A bird locked in a cage won't ever be happy. One day, it'll fly away into oblivion.

This diner where my father waits for me makes me feel like a caged bird. His mere gaze makes me choke on my own breath again.

Nothing has changed.

I shouldn't have answered his desperate call and come here. But I can't turn away now. It's too late; he's already seen me.

What if he has something important to say? What if he's sick or dying?

I don't want to be that jerk who doesn't show up when it's the last time you could ever see each other. When it's the last time a father and daughter could make amends. Everyone desperately wants to love their parents, even the damaged ones. The ones who use and break without a single thought. That's my father in a nutshell ... and for years, I let him.

But not anymore. I'm finally working hard and living on my own without his help, and I'm proud of it.

But no pride reflects in his eyes. Nothing exists except misery and hatred.

"Charlotte," he mumbles, and I bend over to kiss him on the cheeks. "Sit down, we have to talk," he says, and he snaps his fingers at the waitress who glares back at him.

Way to get to the point, Father.

"Hello to you too," I say, chuckling it off.

God, it's been such a long time ago since we last saw each other, and I'm immediately reminded why.

"How are things ... at *work*?" he asks, clearing his throat while he makes it sound as though he doesn't believe I actually work.

"It's fine," I lie.

The truth is that I quit my job as a daycare provider in order to start my own business to support families in need with supplies and advice. I want to do something more fulfilling, but investors are tough to come by ... especially when they don't trust me and my idea. For now, I'm pulling money from my savings account to pay for my rent, but I'm not about to tell him that. Even though it's soon run out, I won't ever ask him for help.

"How's Elijah doing?" I ask, avoiding the topic.

"Your brother? Oh, he's ... well, he's busy, as always," my father says, waving it away. "But enough about that. Do you want some coffee?" Father asks. Before I can answer, he's already ordered my drink for me. "One cappuccino." I don't even like cappuccino, but I'll take it.

"Thanks," I mutter. "So how have *you* been?"

"Awful," he says, slurping his coffee. "Just like this coffee. Don't you have anything better?" he snarls at the waitress.

She shrugs. "Sorry, sir. That's our best blend."

"Bland indeed," he says, rolling his eyes.

"Father," I mutter.

Has he always been like this? Probably. I made him seem better in my mind just to cope.

"No, they should make better coffee," he growls while the waitress places down my cappuccino in front of me.

"Why did you even wanna meet at this place if you don't like it here?" I ask.

"Because it's the only option I had." He clears his throat. "Considering my budget."

"*Budget?*" I frown and lean back in my seat. "Wait, you don't mean to say—"

"The business is not going well," he interjects, but it

sounds as though he's grossly understating things. "But you already knew that. I told you a while ago when I asked you for help."

"Yes," I say, folding my arms, "and I specifically remember saying no."

"I know you did, but listen …" He takes in a deep breath and licks his thin lips. "I'm on the brink of losing everything. I did the only thing I could. I got a loan."

"So? What does that have to do with me?" I ask, not touching my cappuccino. I know where this is going. I'm almost inclined to leave right now, but I don't wanna jump to conclusions too quickly.

"*Everything*," he says. "You're my last hope."

"Really? What about your wife then? Can't she pitch in?" I snort.

"She's left me." He swallows as if he didn't see it coming from a mile away.

I raise a brow. "Let me guess, she ran away with all your money?"

He narrows his eyes at me, but it's all I need.

"Figured." I sigh. "I tried to warn you."

"Charlotte," he says in a condescending tone. "You're my daughter."

"So?" I suck on my bottom lip. He can't play on my emotions, not now.

"A loan always needs to be repaid. And part of the agreement was that you—"

"No," I interrupt, my heart palpitating. "Tell me you

didn't."

He closes his lips and stares me down, which tells me he really did do it.

"No, not happening," I say, shaking my head. "How dare you try this on me again?"

"It's too late. The deal has already been made," he replies.

My heart stops. "What?!"

I get up, and with a flat hand, I slap his face. The whole place has gone quiet, and everybody's looking at us, but I don't care. "I am *not* an object you can trade for money! I'm your *daughter*!"

I refuse to become that woman who belongs to someone like some sort of pet. I want to be independent, someone with her own business and her own life. No man will ever make that happen, and no man can make me as happy as my independence does.

Father reaches for my hand, but I pull it away before he can grab it. "Charlotte, you'll be happy with this man. I promise you."

My father has always tried to control me by telling me what school to go to, how to dress, and what to say. When I didn't listen, he scolded me … sometimes, he even hit me.

And now, he's gone and traded me to some man in exchange for a loan.

"No. You can't say that. You can't do this to me." I shake him off and try to walk away.

Right then, the door to the establishment opens and in

walks a handsome, suited-up man with wavy dark hair, a cleft chin ... *and* an insufferably arrogant grin on his face.

My eyes widen, and I begin to stutter. "Easton ..."

Easton Van Buren ... once a simple waiter in my father's restaurant with big dreams, he's now a notorious business mogul who opens clubs all around the world. We first met at my father's second wedding when we were still kids, and now we meet again ... at what seems to be mine.

"Hello, Charlotte," he muses, his voice still as salacious as I remember. "How nice of you to be here too. Right on time."

No, this can't be happening. Not here ... and not with *him*. Even though he sure looks like James freaking Bond when he walks and talks, I know he has an ulterior motive, and it's anything but good.

He walks toward me and briefly grazes my arm, but the implications are huge.

"You," I mutter in complete shock. "Why are you ...?"

He licks his lips, and a wicked smile forms on his face. But those eyes ... those dazzling blue eyes only show contempt and vengeance.

"No," I mutter.

"Yes," he murmurs. "*I'm* the one who lent money to your father, and I want *you* as payment for that debt."

For a few seconds, all I can do is stare. Then my palm instinctively comes up to slap him. However, he grabs my wrist before I can even come close.

"Ah-ah, Charlotte. That's not nice. Hasn't your father

taught you manners?"

I spit in his face. "Asshole."

He wipes off the spit with one hand. "Now, now … it seems I'll have to teach you to behave."

My father clears his throat as if to grab his attention. "I take it you'll accept this agreement then?"

"Oh, yes." The way Easton says it makes the hairs on the back of my neck stand up.

"What?" I mutter. I can't believe this. He honestly sold me to a rich asshole just to get rid of his loan? "I'm not a bargaining chip!" I exclaim. "How dare you?"

Easton grabs my chin, and says, "I dare because I've wanted nothing more than to own you, and now I do." The smirk that follows makes me want to smack him, but I don't think he'd let me.

"I'm not an object. I'm a person, and I don't fucking agree with any of this," I hiss, glaring right back at him, so he knows I mean it.

"Tsk … we'll have to do something about that dirty mouth of yours," he growls, licking his lips. "And I know just the thing."

He grabs my wrist and drags me toward the door.

"Let go of me!" I yell, punching his arm, but he's too strong for me.

"No, Charlotte," he says. "You're mine now to do with as I please."

"Are you insane? Do you think you'll get away with this?" I stare him down. "You don't scare me."

My eyes widen as he lifts up his shirt to reveal a gun.

"Do I scare you now?" he murmurs.

When I nod, a grin spreads on his lips that remind me of the devil.

"Good," he says. "Now ... don't make a scene, and do as I say, and no one will be harmed."

"You're trying to sell me! Please, Father!" I call out as a final plea for help.

But my father ignores it. "Charlotte, do your duty to your family."

I glance at the waitress, the only other person in this diner, but she completely ignores us. Easton probably paid her off to keep quiet.

"Charlotte ..." Father adds. "Do this. For me. Please."

That last word hits me hard, and I stop fighting Easton. My lungs suck the air in and out like no tomorrow as I gaze into my father's sincere eyes. He's never begged me for anything. This is the first ... and probably the last time.

Easton leans toward me, whispering dark words into my ear. "Your father sold his soul to his company, and he paid the ultimate price."

"What do you mean?" I mutter.

"The only way to pay it off was with you ... Or with his life."

My eyes widen as I face the guilt laced in my father's eyes. He's never looked at me like that ... like he owes me his world. But he does. And now I have to pay with mine.

"No," I whisper, tears welling up in my eyes. "His life or

mine? No, I can't do this. Don't ask me to do this, please," I beg my father, but he looks away in defeat.

My knees buckle, and I have to fight not to sink to the floor.

"Look at it this way," Easton muses, holding me tight. "At least now you'll both live, and you get to say you saved your father's life."

I shake my head. I can't believe Easton's doing this. How did such a sweet, innocent boy become such an evil man? "You're a monster."

His tongue slips out to wet his picture-perfect lips. "Don't worry, Charlotte … This monster will take good care of you." He drags me out of the establishment. "Now let's go home."

TWO

EASTON

After years of waiting and plotting, Charlotte Davis now belongs to me.

I'm surprised by how easily I could convince her father to give her up. With a little bit of pushing and the obvious threat to his life, he surrendered her as if it were no big deal.

But it is to me. She's my little treasure to keep and use however I see fit.

A long time ago, at her father's wedding, that girl stole my heart ... and then stomped on it with her two-thousand dollar high heels a few years later.

I'll prove to her how good I can be. I can't fucking wait to get my hands all over her. I wonder if anyone's touched her, if she's kissed a man before … if she's still a virgin.

That *was* one of the deal breakers for me, and her father knows this, so I hope he was right when he said he's kept her away from other men for most of her life. It's unfortunate I could only get to her after so much time had passed. I would've stolen her away from that wretched man long ago if I could have, but I simply didn't have the leverage then that I do now.

And she *will* know the power I've accumulated.

A simple glance her way makes her cower in fear as she sits next to me in my car. She's still looking at me like I'm the devil incarnate.

Sweet, innocent, gullible Charlotte … she doesn't even know how lucky she is. There's nothing to fear. I'll treat her like the princess she thinks she is, and then I'll make her grovel and beg me to pluck her cherry. Will she taste sweet or sour? I can't fucking wait to find out.

But first, we need to eat. I'm famished. I haven't eaten anything since I got off the plane. I had to come all the way from the Netherlands to the United States just to claim my end of the deal … her.

And now that I have her, I can't wait to take her back to my home and ravage her night after night. But we should fill our stomachs first because we have a long trip ahead of us.

When the car parks outside the restaurant, I clear my throat and wait until she looks at me. She hasn't spoken a word since I forced her into the car, but I'm sure she has a lot of questions.

I haven't decided whether I'll answer them, but she hasn't even tried to ask any. Maybe she'll loosen up once we've eaten. I'm sure she's hungry as it looked like her father didn't give her anything to eat.

"We're here," I say. "Let's eat."

I step out of the car and lock it before going to the other side and opening it up for her. I told the driver to stay inside at all times because I want him available and ready to go. I also want to make sure she doesn't go anywhere should she try to run.

He knows not to mess with me, just like all my other staff. They've been trained from the start to be quiet and respect my authority. It's the only way they get paid their ample salary and ensure their families remain safe.

Threats always work to get what I want, and I don't fucking regret any of them. I've worked too hard for my wealth and power to let anyone touch it. I don't care what anyone thinks of that. I take what I want, and I own it. Fully. Completely. Just like her.

I don't want her because it's *her*, because she's so witty, or charming, or cute.

No, I want her so I can control her. So I can use her for my every desire and make her bend to my will. I'll flaunt her submission in her father's face as the ultimate revenge.

Fuck, I can't wait to see the tears on that fucker's face.

It was already magnificent seeing their eyes connect the moment he gave her away, how her face turned white with betrayal and his filled with wrenching guilt. I could have come right there and then just from watching her squirm.

Yes, I'm an evil son of a bitch, but I don't care.

That man made me into the monster I am today.

Because of him, *my* father is dead ... and he *will* pay.

Licking my lips, I glare at her sitting in the car. Her legs are crossed, and her arms are folded as she gazes out the other window where I was just seated only seconds ago. She can avoid me all she wants, but sooner or later, she's gonna have to come to terms with what her father did. What he gave away—his supposed precious little girl—is now mine to seduce and possess.

"Are you gonna get out?" I ask.

"No," she hisses.

"Do you want me to drag you like I did in that restaurant?" I narrow my eyes. "Because I will if I have to."

She sighs and then steps out, bumping into me rudely. I know she's trying to prove a point, but it doesn't faze me. She'll do exactly what I ask her to do because my threats aren't just threats ... I follow through. And I think she knows that right about now.

I hold out my arm in an attempt to remain civil, and she reluctantly takes it. Still, she refuses to even look at me. It's okay ... we'll get to that part later when she's on her knees.

I lean in sideways until my lips graze her ears. "Do not try to escape or talk to anyone. It will get you killed." Her fingers dig into my skin as I speak the words. "If you behave, I'll treat you right," I whisper.

She sucks in a sharp breath. "What are we going to do?"

Isn't the answer obvious? I don't know why she asks. "Eat."

"And then what?" The arrogance in her voice amuses me.

"You'll see," I murmur, the corners of my mouth tipping up. "Come."

I lead her into the restaurant and toward a table, then gesture for her to sit down across from me on a comfy leather couch. It's a high-end establishment, unlike where we were with her father. I wanted it to serve as a nice contrast of what I can offer as opposed to what he's given her all these years.

"Do you like the place?" I ask, unfolding a napkin.

"No," she says bluntly. "When will you let me go?"

I laugh. "Really, Charlotte? You're already talking about freedom?" I shake my head. "We haven't even gotten our food yet. Let's eat first, and then we can talk."

"No, let's talk now," she says, sitting back with her arms crossed again in defiance. "Did you seriously think I'd accept this?"

"As a matter of fact, yes," I say, clearing my throat when the waiter arrives with two plates of giant lobster. "Thank you."

She ignores her food completely, focusing only on me. "What did my father promise you?"

"You," I reply, cutting into my lobster to take a bite.

"He'd never agree to that up front," she hisses. "I don't believe it."

"Maybe he did, or maybe he didn't. It doesn't change the fact that you're here *now,* and that you're *mine.*"

"I don't belong to anyone," she replies, staring down at her lobster as if it's poisonous.

"We're not leaving until you eat that," I say, pointing at her food.

"I don't care."

"Would you say the same if your father died?"

Her eyes widen. I knew she'd still have a weak spot for him.

Oh, Charlotte ... you're too sweet and gullible. That old rat has used you, and now he's thrown you to the wolves, and you still care about him. It's admirable ... but stupid.

"Is that it? That's what you're going to dangle over *my* head?" she asks, resentment showing in her eyes.

Yes. Yes, I fucking am. Because my father died for hers. And I *will* hold the Davis family accountable.

"If you give me no choice, then I will." I add a smile to be nice because I honestly want to be. Sometimes I can be. But not right now because she needs to learn her place first.

"Great," she says, rolling her eyes.

"Look at it this way ... you get to save a life," I say.

"By sacrificing my own," she replies through gritted teeth.

"I promise you I'll make it worthwhile. You'll like it so much you won't ever want to leave." Oh, how I'll make it worth her while.

"You're sick," she snarls, turning her head away.

"Maybe or maybe I'm just infatuated with you," I say. Though she is right ... on some levels, I can be a sick, twisted bastard. "But it's not me who caused this; it's you."

"How? What did I do to deserve this?"

"You know what you did," I growl. "Now eat your lobster."

After I raise my brow, she reluctantly cuts off a piece and stuffs it into her mouth. It takes her a while to swallow, but I watch her every movement and relish the moment she does. It makes me think of all the dirty things I'll make her do when we're alone.

"Why did my father need *your* money? He could've picked anyone who didn't have such an outrageous counteroffer," she suddenly says. "Why you?"

I look up, confused. "He didn't tell you?"

Her nostrils flare as if she's angry with me for her father not talking to her. But that's never been different, and she's ignorant if she can't see that. "No," she replies. "He never included me in his decision-making about the company."

I finish the last bit of my lobster, and say, "The other investors all lost their money. Your father's company went bankrupt."

Her eyes widen. "Bankrupt?"

I'm guessing he never told her that either. "His wife stole everything. But I want assurance that I get my investment back."

"So I'm the bond ..." she says, gazing at her lobster as if it's staring straight back at her.

"Yes, Charlotte. But I never wanted anything else but you."

"As what? A wife?" she jests as she stabs a piece of lobster with her fork and swallows it down.

But this is no laughing matter. I'm serious. Dead serious. And when she realizes I'm not laughing with her, her pupils dilate, and her face turns completely white.

After she swallows, I reply, "Yes. You'll become my wife."

THREE

Charlotte

9 Years Ago

I've never been to a wedding before, but if they're all as pretty as my father's, I'd attend them all. I'm not sure people would allow me to come, though, since I'm not their kid, but if I smiled real cute, I probably could.

Most stuff I get away with. My father's usually too busy with work or one of his girlfriends to even notice I exist. Right now, it's his soon-to-be wife. She brought her own maids of honor, so I wasn't needed. Not that I care. I'd much rather sit here in the audience than be over there in the limelight next to my brother, Elijah, who's beaming as the best man. He likes that the suit gets him a lot of attention, but I'm the opposite of that. I'd much rather be on my own, though that's impossible attending a wedding of this magnitude.

It's over the top. Father flew us all out to the Netherlands just to have the wedding here in Amsterdam. It's his favorite city, so that was all the reason he needed. He had all the Dutch folk set everything up for the ceremony while he sat back in his mansion in the United States. When we flew here just a few days ago, everything was ready to go. I'm surprised he didn't plan his honeymoon here in the Netherlands too. I mean, all that grass and the houses here are beautiful, but their language is so hard to understand, and it's always raining in this flat land. I don't get why my father loves it here so much.

I don't get a lot of things my father does. Like this lady, for example … she's not at all his type. Way too uptight with too much plastic surgery—not to mention, she wasn't here when he built his business from the ground up. She's probably after his money but try telling him that.

Sighing, I look away, and my eyes fixate on a boy standing beside another adult man near the exit. They're watching the spectacle, just as I should be, but I'm far more interested in what they're doing here. Are they friends of my father's? Or do they work for the wedding coordinator?

The man has placed a hand on the boy's shoulder while they both watch my father and his new wife. I don't care about the ceremony. I mean, I love my father, but this new lady ... ugh.

I don't consider her my mom, so she'd better not ask me to call her that. I'll ask my father about it after the wedding. He usually does what I ask as long as it isn't too outrageous.

It comes with the territory of having a father who's barely around. He tries to make up for it with gifts and says yes to literally everything to pretend he's a good father. I'm used to it. I've never known any other life, so I just smile and shrug it off. Things were the same when my mom was still alive, so I don't expect anything to change now that my father's marrying his next wife.

I'm surprised she managed to persuade him to get married. My father's normally very protective of his life because of his multi-million-dollar business. He's smart to shield himself from the gold diggers. I'd probably do the same if I was in charge.

But I won't ever be. I already know my father prefers my brother to continue the business, Davis Holding, in his stead. He's said multiple times that he thinks Elijah is the smarter one, and he's always taking him on business trips while leaving me at home.

I don't mind. I don't like that he makes his preference so obvious, but I do like the freedom it gives me. I get to do whatever I wanna do when I'm old enough. Maybe I'll go on a world trip ... or maybe I'll start my own business and build it from the ground up.

Or maybe I'll end up marrying that handsome boy standing in the corner. He's been staring at me nonstop since I sat down here.

I can't keep my eyes off him even though the heat rises to my cheeks. With that long face, those ocean blue eyes, that cleft chin, and chestnut brown hair, he's so handsome … and he's only a teen.

I wonder what he'll look like when he's an adult. Not that I'll ever see him again. We live in the States, and from the looks of it, he lives here in the Netherlands. He's wearing simple denim jeans, and his father's wearing an apron. Perhaps he's the caterer, and his son just wanted to watch the ceremony, I suppose.

Who wouldn't when it's *this* extravagant with mountains of expensive roses and diamonds everywhere. Hell, I'm sure my father even got golden plates and cutlery, knowing the lady he's currently giving half his fortune too. She loves everything over the top, including herself, and it makes me wanna barf.

When the two exchange the rings and a sloppy kiss, the whole room starts clapping, and so do I … even though I'm not at all happy with his choice. But if my father is happy, then so am I.

After the newlywed couple happily walks down the aisle, we all make our way outside to the beautiful courtyard where we'll have cocktails. Well, the adults will anyway. I'm already happy with a lemon Coke on the rocks.

The first thing I do is run up to the drinks table. I can't

help but grin when I spot that same boy who was staring at me mere minutes ago standing behind the table, pouring drinks into the glasses.

"Hey," he says when I give him an awkward stare.

A blush appears on my face, and I tuck a strand of my hair behind my ear. "Hi ..."

"One, two, or three?" he asks.

My lips part, but I have no clue what he just asked me. "Um ..."

He points at the prefilled glasses. "Coke, iced tea, and orange juice."

I narrow my eyes. "So there isn't an option to ... mix?"

"Sure, which ones do you want mixed?" he asks, flipping the bottle as though it means nothing and he does this all the time like a true pro. He winks, making my heart flutter. But then I have to stop him from actually pouring two of them into one cup.

"No, I mean ... a Coke with lemon? Maybe?" I bite my lip.

He cocks his head. "We don't normally add those ... but I'll make one for you," he says, and his lip curls up in such a sexy way that it almost makes my heart jump out of my chest.

Geez, Charlotte, get a grip.

"One lemon Coke, coming right up," he says while flipping the bottle and then fishing a slice of lemon from his fridge. He sure is slick with this whole thing.

"You do this often, don't you?" I ask. "Isn't that like ...

child labor or something?"

He laughs. "I'm sixteen. Old enough to work part-time," he says with a smirk. "Besides, I'm on vacation right now, so I might as well earn some money."

I feel like a fool for even saying something.

He looks over my shoulder at a man standing behind a large table filled with delicious cakes and pies. "I help my father out with the catering when he needs it."

"Interesting." I nod a few times, impressed. "You know, you speak excellent English for a Dutchman."

"Oh, I'm not Dutch," he replies.

"Whoops, sorry," I say, clearing my throat. "I shouldn't have assumed—"

"It's fine. We only just moved here from the US," he says, shrugging. "Business opportunities or something."

"Awesome. We're only here for the wedding, but I can't imagine having to learn the language."

"Ah, it's not so bad. Besides, my father teaches me. He grew up here." He scratches the back of his head. "But I'm still getting used to it."

"Hope your father pays you well then. You deserve it, especially with those amazing flips," I say.

A mischievous smile curls his lips. "A little more than he should, but I usually tuck half back into his wallet when he isn't looking."

"Wow. Not only a great host, but also the best son a father could want," I say, and his charming smile makes me swoon. He's such a cutie and so nice too. My father should definitely hire him more often. And his father, of course. Can't forget about him.

"So … what's your name?" he suddenly asks.

"Oh, Charlotte, hehe." I tuck a strand of my hair behind my ear. I deliberately don't tell him my last name because I don't want him to know that pompous man who just got married is *my* father.

"Easton Van Buren," he says, and he holds out his hand. "Nice to meet you."

We shake hands and end it with an awkward smile. Luckily, he immediately hands me my drink because I wouldn't wanna be caught fidgeting.

"Boring wedding, right?" he mutters under his breath, laughing it off a little.

"Yeah," I reply, trying not to make it sound as though I actually know these people even though I do. Too well. I wish that wasn't the case right now because this is embarrassing.

"If I had that much money, I wouldn't spend it on any wedding. I'd cruise the world, or build my own home, or start a whole chain of clubs, or create a charity fund," he says.

I take a few sips of my Coke. "A charity fund? For?"

"Children in poverty," he says. "But you know… no one gives a shit about charities like that," he says while chopping ice to put into the glasses.

"I do," I say, clutching my glass.

He stops picking the ice and cocks his head. "Really? Or

are you just saying that to sound cool?" He raises a brow.

"Nah, I mean it," I reply, taking another sip of my drink.

"So if you were rich, you'd donate money to my hypothetical charity?" He puts up a smug face that makes it hard to say no.

So I nod. "I would," I say. "But only if you swear on it that you'd do the same."

"Fine," he says, holding out his hand. "I'll swear on it."

Damn, he's serious about this.

I grab his hand and shake it again. "Deal."

His grin is infectious. "Now all we need to know is which of us will get rich first."

I try to contain my laughter, but it's hard. I don't want him to think I'm a douche. I mean, if I was rich, I would do it. But my father's the wealthy one, and I'm not sure he'd ever spend it on a charity.

"That prick who's getting married right now doesn't give a shit about any of that, I'm pretty sure. You're the first who's shown any interest in talking with any of the staff."

"The only one? I doubt that." I narrow my eyes, ignoring the fact he just called my father a prick.

"Literally the case. No offense," he says. "I mean, I don't wanna be an asshole, but you know how rich people are …"

I rub my lips together, not knowing how to answer that.

"Charlotte!" My father's voice immediately makes me turn my head. He beckons me to come over. "Ahh …" I mutter when Easton's eyes travel toward my father.

The one who got married is *my* father. And I'm the spoiled, rich daughter.

His smile slowly dissipates.

Our eyes connect again, and at that moment, he knows what I think of him. That he was a dick for insulting my father, but I don't even mind because he's right. In his eyes, I'm that filthy rich girl who could do everything she wanted, and the world envies people like me. But they don't know what goes on behind closed doors and how we miss things like human interaction and actual love.

And even though I'd love for nothing more, we'll probably never talk again. Our worlds are too different, too far apart for that to ever happen.

"Shit," he stammers. "I didn't … I wasn't …"

"I know," I say, smiling it off as if it means nothing. "My father's a dick."

He grimaces. "I probably shouldn't have said that."

"It's the truth. I should know," I reply. "Besides, you know how rich people are." I wink, but that doesn't make the hurt any less.

I wish my father hadn't called out my name, so we could've continued this pretty little lie until the end of the night. At least then this wedding might've been fun.

"If it makes it any better, I don't think you're like that at all," he adds, clearing his throat.

"Like what? An asshole who cares only about money?"

He licks his lips and looks down at the glasses he was pouring. "I apologize. If I'd known he was your father,

I'd—"

"No. I want to know what people think of him," I say, taking another sip of my Coke. "Makes for some fun conversations, that's for sure."

I put down the glass and take a deep breath when my father calls me again, this time a little harsher. "Charlotte! Come here!"

I sigh out loud. "Good luck with work today," I say, turning around.

"Have fun," he says, and I can't help but notice the contempt in his voice.

I don't blame him. I'd feel cheated too. "Thanks," I say, trying to add a smile, but it's not genuine.

"I hope your father's new wife is nice to you. You deserve it," he adds after I've already started walking. "I promise next time I won't be such an asshole!"

Shaking my head, I laugh and yell back at him over my shoulder, "You'd better not!"

Then I walk back to my father, whose penetrative stare could cut through mountains. The few steps there feel like a walk of shame because he seems royally pissed. "Could you have taken any longer? Aren't you going to congratulate us?" He gives me the stink eye.

"Okay …" Elijah mutters, standing beside my father. "Awkward." He always watches as I'm about to get my ass handed to me. He never intervenes even though I often look him directly in the eyes. Just as I am now. All he does is turn around and walk off, not wanting to get in the middle of it.

Typical.

Rolling my eyes, I kiss my father's and his new wife's cheeks. "Congratulations."

"Thank you, darling," she says, making my skin crawl.

"What the hell were you doing there?" my father asks. "Chatting up that lowlife?"

"He's not a lowlife, Father," I say, making a face.

"His father's a caterer. You have no business talking to a boy like that."

I despise how judgmental my father can be sometimes. As if no one's ever good enough for him. "I can talk to whoever I want."

He grabs my wrist and forces me to come closer. "Charlotte, stop acting like a little brat."

He's making a scene now, and everybody's watching. I'm being humiliated in front of all the guests.

"I'm not a brat! Stop calling me that." I jerk free of his grip, and say, "I can do whatever I want. You can't control me."

Suddenly, he smacks me across the face. Right in front of everyone.

My face stings when tears roll down the red mark he left on my cheek.

"How dare you? You're ruining this perfect wedding. Behave."

"You hit me," I mumble, touching my cheek.

"That's what you get for acting out. You listen to me when I tell you not to talk to someone, Charlotte." He points at my chest as if his finger adds extra weight to his words. It sure feels like it. "Don't ever embarrass me like that again."

My father and his new wife turn around and walk up to the guests. "Now, where's the music? It's time for our first dance."

Everyone starts smiling again, and they all walk away toward the staged area while I'm left with my head hanging between my shoulders.

His embarrassment ... that's all that matters to him. His image. His pride.

And I tarnished that idea by even being remotely interested in someone who's beneath us. Because that's what he thinks when he looks at someone like Easton. Just a worker who should keep his mouth shut.

But that's not what I see when I look at him right now. The pity and empathy he exudes from one look are enough to make me cry even harder. I don't deserve any of that compassion or that sincerity that encompasses him.

And when he parts his lips to say something from across the terrain, I spin on my heels and run off.

***

Charlotte

Present

I once met a boy at a wedding party. It was a picturesque location with the prettiest of decorations, but under the pressure of money, it all fell flat ... except for him. That boy who managed to lighten my mood even when I was feeling down because of my father's choice to marry his shiny new plastic wife.

I never understood why I was so enamored with talking to that boy or why I was so attracted to him. Maybe I wished for my life to be as simple as his seemed to be. Maybe I wished for a father like his instead of mine, who would rather slap me and give me away than love me.

Or maybe I wished for that same boy to whisk me away into a prettier life.

But I never expected any of those wishes to come to fruition.

Now I'm stuck in a restaurant with that same boy who's now a full-fledged man, complete with a chiseled body and a smirk that makes girls' knees buckle.

It does nothing for me. Taken against my will, I was just a pawn in a grand scheme to destroy my father's empire. And now he expects me to marry him too as a payment toward my father's debt.

No freaking way.

I can't believe I ever fawned over this guy or even liked him as a boy. Look at what he's become. All rich men are the same. Once they have cash, they behave like animals, devouring anything they come across. And now it's my turn.

I don't intend to become his wife. But I can't run away from him either because I don't want to have the murder of my father on my conscience. My father may be a giant asshole, but he's still my father, and I still care about him. Despite him treating me badly all my life, I don't want him to die.

My father would never risk his life for money. Did my father go to him, or was it the other way around? Maybe Easton was after me all this time. "Tell me, honestly, did you give my father that loan *just* to get to me?"

The wicked grin that spreads on his face speaks volumes. "Not only a pretty fucking princess but a smart one too."

My skin crawls. I don't want to believe it, but I have to. All these years after the wedding, he was still obsessed with me. Why, I don't know because we barely spoke and only on a handful of occasions. But my father forbade it in an instant, and that was that. But I guess Easton didn't take it so well.

"So you *wanted* his business to fail. Did you set him up?"

"No, that was all on him," he replies.

"How much did you offer him?" I ask, feeling resentful

of the price tag on my head.

"Twenty million."

My jaw drops, and I try my hardest not to let him see, but I'm already too late, judging from the devilish gleam in his eyes.

"And you'd be worth far more than that, but I didn't want to give your father more cash than he deserved," he muses, trying to grab my hand, but I remove it from the table. "I'll give you the world if you let me."

"No way," I hiss.

"You're only saying that because you're overwhelmed. But you'll change your mind soon enough," he says, getting up from his chair.

"I doubt that," I say, but he clears his throat as if he doesn't wanna hear me.

"C'mon. We're leaving," he says.

I make a face. "Where are you taking me now? Another fancy trip? Wanna flaunt me like some goddamn prize?"

He pulls me out of my seat and wraps his arm firmly around my waist, forcing me to leave with him.

"My home ... and I promise, you'll love it there. You won't ever want to go back once you're there."

"*There?*" That sounds far. "Back from where?" I ask as he drags me outside where the car waits.

He opens the door, and growls, "The Netherlands." And before I can say another word, he pushes me into the car and shuts the door.

FOUR

Charlotte

I've thought of escaping. At every turn, every time I stepped out of a car, moved through a hallway, walked into a new door … I've thought about running away.

But then that image of my father's dead body in a casket pops up, and I hesitate. And then the moment passes.

That's how it's been for the past few hours as I was escorted to the airstrip.

Within minutes, we're in a private jet that lifts off and flies over the horizon. Everything happens faster than I can process. How did I let all of this happen?

Easton threatened my father's life ... but would he really do it? Would he honestly have my father killed just to prove his point? Who would be that cruel?

This man staring at me from his seat right across from me. This man keeping me as a hostage for his pleasure.

Why does he want me so badly? We barely know each other, and we've only seen each other a couple of times.

"What are you thinking about?" he suddenly asks, interrupting my train of thought.

I shift in my seat and take a deep breath. "What did I do to make you want me so badly? What's so special about me?"

His index finger rests just below his lips, framing the smile that appears. "Everything."

The smug look on his face makes me flush. I shouldn't because it's not right, but no one ever says these things straight to my face, and I don't know what to do about it.

"You should feel flattered that I want you," he adds.

But all it just makes me want to gag. My stomach twists as though someone's wrapped a rope around me and pulls tighter and tighter until I can no longer breathe.

Suffocation. That's how it feels ... Like being confined to a chest by a man who only takes me out when it's time for play.

A shiver rolls up and down my spine at the thought of what that playtime will be like. What does he plan on doing with me once we're married? And when the time comes, will I be able to thwart him off?

I look out the window as we cross the ocean, and I mentally say goodbye to the country I used to call mine. It feels as though I'll never set foot there again.

But I won't let this man get to me because surely, this won't last forever. One way or another, that debt will be repaid, and then I'll be free. I won't have to pay for my father's reckless spending, right? He knows it wasn't my fault, so I'm sure he's working on a different solution as we speak.

"Are you daydreaming?" Easton asks.

I shift in my seat, trying to ignore him, but it's hard with his penetrative stare constantly on my face.

"You know you can speak, right?" he says.

"I don't see the need," I reply, glancing at him for only a second, but it's already too much because just the sight of his deep blue eyes has my body quaking.

God, why does he have this effect on me? I hate it.

"Of course, you do. I know you have questions," he says, "but you're too afraid to ask. I won't bite, I promise … not hard anyway." The smirk that follows heats me to my core.

"Is that what this is, why you chose me?" I ask, trying not to let my guard down. "So you could act out all your filthy fantasies on me?"

His thumb brushes along his lip softly. "Perhaps." There's a short pause. "But you know damn well why …"

"Enlighten me," I say, tilting my head and pretending I don't know.

I know he loaned my father money, but I don't know how the two even came into contact, knowing where Easton came from. My father must've been impressed with his company.

But I can't believe he'd offer up his daughter as a failsafe. Did my father know Easton wanted me all along, or did Easton suggest it?

Maybe my father never intended to pay back the loan in the first place, and this was all part of his plan to get rid of me. Or maybe Easton made sure my father could never pay it off so he could get his hands on me.

Damn ... there's so much I don't know. I'm dying to ask my father, but there's no way I'll ever be able to contact him with Easton breathing down my neck. And not only that, but I doubt my father would answer my questions. His pride is too big for him to swallow and tell me the truth. If he had to choose between his pride or his life, he'd probably choose to die instead.

That's how stubborn he is. But I'm not. I don't want him to die. Despite our very rocky relationship, he's still my father, and I care about him.

"Hmm ..." Easton chuckles a little. I hate the sound. Hate it with every breath of my life. "I said I know you had questions. I never said I'd answer all of them."

I sigh out loud. "Then why dangle the suggestion in front of me?"

"Because it's fun to see you squirm," he jests, shrugging as if it means nothing.

Fuck him. He's making fun of me now.

"Ah, finally," he says when a woman walks toward us while holding a tray with two champagne glasses. "Thank you." He grabs two and places one on the table next to me, sliding it toward me.

"No, thanks," I say without even acknowledging him or the drink.

"C'mon, I know you want to."

"I'd prefer not to get intoxicated around dangerous men," I say with a snide undertone. "Next thing you know, they'll take you hostage and tie you to their bed."

He snorts, and a lopsided grin spreads across his lips. "I love how filthy your mind is. That will come in handy when it's time to get down and dirty."

"Dream on," I snap.

"Oh, I haven't shown you how bad I can get, Charlotte … and I won't just tie you up to my bed," he says, leaning forward as if to instill fear into me just by coming closer. "I'll make you beg for it until you scream my name from pure pleasure."

I swallow away the lump in my throat and cross my legs because it suddenly feels like I have no panties on even though I do. "That'll never happen."

"Of course, it will," he answers. "Once you're my wife, it'll happen every … single … day."

My legs clench together at the thought, my heart beating in my throat. I have to stop letting him get to me so much because he's nothing but an evil bastard. I have to get rid of that image in my mind of that young boy who was once so nice to me. Where has that boy gone?

"And here I was, thinking you were such a nice guy way back when we first met. Guess I was wrong," I say, holding my head up high.

"People change, Charlotte. You, of all people, should know that." He raises his brow.

"I thought you were a better man," I murmur.

His laughter dies off painfully slow. "So did I … once," he muses.

"Let me guess, you blame me?" I raise a brow.

His eyes become thin slits. "Yes … and you know damn well why."

***

EASTON

7 Years Ago

"So you mix the two fluids, and then you add the dry ingredients. Got it?" my father says as he makes a smooth puree. I never understood any of this cooking stuff, and I've always been horrible in the kitchen, but I wanna learn. My father's a great cook, and I envy his ability to quickly adapt. Whenever I'm behind a stove, I just burn everything. But I wanna make him happy.

I'm more adept at serving customers, and I think my father knows that because he always puts me on the waiter jobs whenever we work together. When the people who hire him approve, of course. Many people hire him because they all want to make use of his great cooking skills.

Me, I'm just glad I finished high school, but I have no clue what the hell I wanna do. My father keeps saying I should take over his business, and I suppose he's right. It'd be a waste to let all his hard work slip when he retires. He built his business from the ground up over the years, and I'm proud of that. I'm just not sure if this is my thing.

"Do you get it or not?" he asks again.

Pulled from my train of thought, I mutter, "Ah, yeah, of course, I get it."

"Tsk. Stop lying, Easton. You always do that." He sighs. "Go serve them this."

He puts three glasses filled with puree on a tray and shoos me out of the kitchen. He only works part-time for this restaurant, but it's already pulled in some peculiar customers. Mostly rich people yearning to try out my father's creations. He's like a magician with food while I'm … just me. All I'm good at is flipping bottles and making some cool-looking drinks. But those things don't make you money. You can't build a career on drinks. Right?

I need to get my shit together and focus on what's important; learning the best of my father's skills so I can apply them when he retires and I take over his business. Working hard is the key.

With the tray in my hand and a clean cloth in the other, I march out the door and put on my best smile. However, the moment I notice who our guests are, my smile immediately disappears.

It's her... that girl from that over-the-top wedding years ago.

Charlotte Davis.

I'd recognize her anywhere.

She has such distinct green eyes and a smile that anyone would be envious of. Not to mention the pink hair, which is hard to miss. As is her long, white dress ... and tits that are tightly strapped inside.

Fuck. She grew up fast.

I still try to give her a courteous smile and let her know I recognize her, but she won't even spare me one glance. All she does is stare out the window and ignore everyone around her. Fucking rude ... but I guess that's how these rich folks are.

"Compliments of the house," I mutter as I set the tiny glasses in front of them.

She still won't acknowledge me. It's as if I don't even exist. Has she forgotten about me already? Or is this because of her father?

I clearly remember the way he treated her at his wedding, how he slapped her in front of everyone and let her cry all by herself. When she ran off to the bathroom, I wanted to follow her, but then it hit me that the only reason it happened was because she'd talked to me.

Maybe that's why she's ignoring me on purpose right now. She doesn't wanna get hurt again.

"Thanks, boy," her father says. He sips the juice from the glass. "Delicious. As always." He takes in a deep breath as if he's savoring it. "Boy, call out the chef, will you? I need to speak with him."

"I'm sorry, sir. I would, but he's busy making dinner. Our guests will be here any moment."

"Are you sure you want to take a real opportunity away from your father?" he says, lifting a brow. "I'm sure your father won't be happy with you making that decision."

I don't like the way he's looking at me, nor his tone. But I sigh and do what he wants because that's my job. "I'll go get him right away, sir."

I turn around and walk back to the kitchen. My father immediately bombards me with questions. "And? What did they say? Did they enjoy it? What did his face look like?"

"He loved it. Said it was delicious. He looked like he was savoring the taste," I reply, trying to forget the fact that *she's* out there too. "He wants to talk to you."

"Oh?" My father places his hand on his chest. "I'm flattered. Can you take over back here for a sec?"

"Sure," I say as he walks out. I swallow away the lump in my throat and stare at the food. Then I open the door a little bit and peek through the opening. I know it's wrong to listen to their conversation, but my curiosity gets the best of me.

"I want you to work for me."

"Wait, really?"

"Really. I'll give you your own restaurant. Head chef. Full time. Name your price."

Wow. This guy's offering my father his dream job. But I'm not sure I'm happy about that. The last time we met him, he didn't exactly make a great impression. All he's got going for him is that he has multiple restaurants and hotels across the world under his name, or so I've heard. I don't doubt my father's happy about this opportunity, but I just hope her father doesn't abuse mine.

When my father comes back, he seems over the moon. However, the moment he looks at me, his smile vanishes. "What is it?" I ask.

"He offered me a job, but he wants me to do everything without you."

"Why? What did I do?" I frown, offended that he's singling me out.

"Well, since his daughter will be around too, and she often comes to the restaurants he owns, he doesn't want her to interact with you."

"You mean he's afraid I'll try to flirt with her?" I say through gritted teeth.

"Well, he didn't put it like that, but—"

"Don't even try to explain it," I say, holding up my hand. "And you're okay with this? Me losing my part-time job?"

"Well, there's plenty of other work you could do," he says, trying to grab me, but I immediately pull away.

"I liked this. I liked working with you," I say. "I can talk to him. Maybe he'll change his mind."

"No, wait!" my father yells as I march out the door.

He's too late to stop me. I'm already by their table before he's even clutched the door. I don't care if he watches.

"Why do you want me gone?" I ask Davis bluntly.

He looks up with an arrogant smirk on his face. "Excuse me, who are you?"

"I'm *his* son," I say, clenching my fists together. "Why can't I continue working with my father?"

Davis just laughs at me.

I grind my teeth. "What's so funny?"

With a condescending look on his face, he says, "The fact that you think what you do is work."

Fuck him and the fucking horse he thinks he rode in on. It takes all my patience right now not to sucker-punch this fucker out of the restaurant.

"My father and I are a team. We've *always* worked together."

His face darkens. "And now that's going to change."

"What's your problem?" I ask, cocking my head.

"My problem is you trying to talk it up with my daughter," he hisses.

Wait ... Charlotte's the reason I'm getting *fired*? I make a face. "You think I'm going to flirt with *her*?"

The sudden mention of the word *her* has caught her attention. She briefly glances my way, and at that moment of pure hatred, our eyes connect. But I don't see the same happy, smart girl I once saw. All I see is gloom and the wish for things to end quickly. As if she pities me.

And it only makes me want to grab their glasses and smash them to the ground.

I'm not the one who needs pity. She is.

But she immediately looks away and stares out the window as if I've ceased to exist. As if we never even talked at her father's wedding and she doesn't remember me. But I *know* she does. I could see it in her eyes.

"I *know* you remember me," I say. When she still doesn't speak, I yell, "Look at me!"

I want her to know that I won't let her forget me. That her father used her to explain the fact I'm losing my job.

Suddenly, her father grabs my wrist, and growls, "Listen to me, you little …" He clears his throat to prevent himself from saying something I'm sure was going to be nasty. "Don't you fucking look or talk to my daughter like that. You will never, ever be good enough for my daughter. You hear me?"

"Father," Charlotte mutters, her eyes widened.

I jerk myself free from his grip. "I never said I wanted—"

"I'm not blind, kid. I know you want her; I saw it with my own eyes. I've known ever since you two had that little chat at my wedding." He points at me with his crooked finger as if it's a gun. "And I'll die before I let that happen."

I swallow, trying to make sense of his words. Is this a

threat or a dare? I can't tell.

"Don't think you ever had a chance to begin with, boy," he adds.

I don't believe him.

"Father!" Charlotte looks mortified. "Please!"

He completely ignores her. "You're just a common busboy. A waiter who'll serve our drinks and that's it. You won't amount to anything more, and she will never, *ever* talk to you again. You hear me?"

My nostrils flare as I glance at both her and her father, but he's the only one who will look me directly in the eyes. It's as though she's too afraid to even try. She's still ignoring me, still pretending I don't exist, and that fucking hurts.

I don't say another word as I grab the two glasses and take them with me back to the kitchen. I won't give him the satisfaction of my response. I won't let them witness my full-blown rage.

Both of them will get their comeuppance one day. I'll make sure of it. And when the time comes, I'll dance on her father's fucking grave.

A stupid smirk spreads across my lips. One day, she *will* belong to me. Whatever it takes. I won't stop until she's mine completely.

And I'll make him witness me kissing her, marrying her … fucking her.

Just so that bastard can see how wrong he was about me.

FIVE

Charlotte

1 Year Ago

The last time I saw Father was probably months ago. I try not to go to his house too often because our conversations always derail into shouting matches about who's right and who's wrong. And I can never, ever win that fight. Especially not with that woman living with him and always taking his side. He protects her more than he ever cared about me.

That's why I decided to move out and live in my own tiny apartment. It's a much safer and saner place to live, and

I have some savings I can live on until I find a job. I haven't gotten one yet, but I know if I keep pushing, I'll be successful. I have to because I'll run out of savings someday, and there's no way I'm going back to my father.

Well, except to check on him, of course. I mean, I can't just let him sit on his golden throne while his wife waits for him to drop dead so she can claim his wealth. That won't be happening on my watch.

My father's never been nice to me, but he's still my father, and I don't want him to be anyone's victim.

Today's our annual get-together with the whole family before he goes on summer vacation, and I went to his place to make sure his wife is still behaving and not secretly poisoning my father. We're all sitting at the table in silence, eating our dinner without even looking at each other.

My father seems to be okay, health-wise, but I'm not sure mentally he's doing so well. He's more absent than usual, and the littlest things, like a misplaced fork or food not being salty enough, enrage him. It's as if something's going on, but he won't tell me.

Suddenly, he slams down his fork and says to the butler, "Can you fucking make sure the steak isn't overcooked this time?"

"Sorry, sir," his new butler apologizes. He's gone through five of them in the past two years. "It won't happen again."

"Better not." My father scoffs, patting his lips with his napkin.

"Father," I mutter, lowering my fork.

"What?" he snarls.

"Charlotte, better not go there," Elijah tries to warn me, but I ignore him.

"Is everything okay? You seem so agitated lately," I say, trying to put it mildly, so Father doesn't get even angrier.

"It's none of your damn business," he growls back.

I frown. "Well, excuse me for being interested." I sigh as I stare out the window.

"Just eat your damn food," he says after a while.

"Not hungry," I reply, grabbing my napkin to wipe my mouth.

"You're only saying that because you're offended," he says.

"I'm not. I'm genuinely worried about you, but you won't talk to me."

"What's there to talk about?" He eyes me down like a vulture. "That you moved out of the house? You constantly ignoring my calls and requests? You constantly ignoring my beautiful wife?" He leans over to touch his wife's hand, and it makes bile rise in my throat.

"I'm not ignoring anyone. I just wanna live on my own as an adult. Is that so wrong?"

"I never said you could move out."

"Yet I did," I reply, shrugging. Apparently, it's hard for my father to realize I'm a full-grown adult now.

"You're *my* daughter," he says as if he still has a say in it.

"So? You let Elijah do whatever he wants." When I look

at Elijah, he gives me this eagle-eyed look. Shaking his head gently, Elijah mouths, "Don't pull me into this."

"Elijah is a responsible young man who can take care of business," my father replies.

"Oh, and I can't?" I narrow my eyes. I knew it. He doesn't trust me. "I've been living on my own just fine," I add.

"On *my* money." He pounds his fist on the table, causing everyone to jolt in their seats. "It's time you learned what responsibility is."

"Yes," I say. "Yes, please. I've been waiting for years for you to involve me in your business. Maybe then I can finally learn something."

"Business?" He scoffs, laughing. Then he returns to his stone-cold killer face again. "No. Elijah will be the one to follow in my footsteps."

I roll my eyes. "Of course, he is." What a surprise. Not.

"Hey, I didn't say he should exclude you," Elijah butts in. "It wasn't my idea."

"No, it was mine," my father says. "I need someone reliable at the wheel."

"Why do you keep saying things just to hurt me?" I ask, tears welling up in my eyes. "Do you enjoy seeing me in pain?"

"No, Charlotte, I don't. But you need to hear the truth, and the truth hurts," he says. "You weren't born to lead."

"Who are you to decide that?" I say through gritted teeth, trying desperately to hold back my tears. I don't wanna shed them for him. No way.

"I decide since I'm the one who's supposed to save this business."

My jaw drops and shock ripples through me. "*Save?*" I murmur. "*Save* the business?"

My father has never said anything about having problems with the business. How long has he been hiding this from us?

However, when I look at Elijah, who's lowered his head while pretending to still eat his dinner, I realize I was the only one who *didn't* know.

"The business is in trouble?" I ask. "And you didn't tell me?"

"Of course not," he replies. "Your brother and I will take care of it."

"But that's your whole life. *Our* lives. All you've ever worked for," I say. Leaning over the table, I try to get him to look at me, but he just keeps cutting into his food. If he goes on any longer, I'm sure there'll be nothing left but mush.

"I know, dammit!" The sudden outburst has him smashing his knife onto the table this time. "I'm well aware of what's at stake."

"Then let me help you," I say in a last desperate attempt to connect.

"You wanna help?" he says, rubbing his napkin over his mouth and then throwing it down on his plate. "Do what I tell you to do."

"Tell me what I need to do," I reply, "and I'll do it."

"Marry a suitor of my choosing."

My eyes widen, and my jaw almost drops to the floor. "*What?*" I laugh it off. He must be joking. Except I'm the only one laughing. "You're kidding, right?"

"The only way to fix this business is if we get another investor on board, and to do that, I need a bargaining chip."

"A *bargaining chip?*" I scoff. I can't believe he's contemplating this. "And you wanna offer me as a reward? Hold on." I grab my glass of water and chug it down in one go. "Like what, go on a date with them?" I'm at a point where I wanna cry, laugh, and yell at the same time. It's that ridiculous.

"As a wife."

The glass I was holding drops to the floor and shatters on impact.

"Wha…?" I can't even form a coherent sentence.

"You'll be able to save the company and the legacy of the Davis name, Charlotte," my father adds as if that will persuade me.

"No," I say when I've finally come to my senses. "No, absolutely not."

Father clears his throat. "I figured you'd say that. But I'm sure you'll change your mind once you see the esteemed men I have in mind."

"Are you insane?" I say, scooting back my chair. "The answer is *no*."

"Charlotte—"

"You've lost your damn mind!" I shout, getting up from my seat. "You think I'll marry some dude I've never met because you wanna save your company?"

"Sit. Down," he growls, practically stabbing me with his eyes.

"No!" I throw my napkin onto the table. "It's *not* happening."

"It is, and you will attend these Meet & Greets."

"Meet & Greets?" I scoff. "So now you've already given them a name? Organized a date?" I shake my head. "I can't believe this. After all this time and all this effort I went through to show interest, to be invested ... *this* is what I get? A father who wants to sell me to the highest bidder?"

"You'll get to know them properly before the time is due for you to pick."

"I won't let you auction off my fucking heart!" I yell.

"Charlotte! Manners!" he yells back.

"I don't care about manners! You don't even care about *me*!" I look at Elijah and beg him with my eyes to do something, but he doesn't even say a word. He's retracted himself from the conversation just to make it easier on himself ... but not on me. Doesn't anyone care?

"Elijah ... please," I ask, but he just looks at me with these apologetic eyes that do nothing for me.

"I'm sorry, sis," he mutters.

"Oh, fuck you all!" I explode.

"Charlotte!" my father yells as I march past him.

"No, I don't give a damn anymore," I hiss, walking

straight to the door.

"Stop right there, young lady!" I can hear his footsteps behind me. "How dare you insult me like this? You're *my* fucking daughter!"

"Yes, Father," I say, spinning on my heels to give him one last piece of my mind. "I'm your daughter. Your *daughter*. A girl you should cherish. Instead, you've given me nothing but pain. And now you want to give me away," I reply. "How dare *you*."

"It's already been arranged," he says as I turn around again.

"I don't care. I'm not going to be there, so good luck," I say, sticking my middle finger up in the air.

"Charlotte! Come back here!" he yells as I stomp out the door and slam it shut behind me.

I don't give a damn what he says or if he even follows me outside. I'm not about to sacrifice my life so he can have his. No way. He may be my father, but he's not responsible for my life any longer. I will make it on my own, and I will not let anyone dictate my life for me.

***

Charlotte

Present

This flight is taking forever.

Easton takes a sip of his champagne. "We'll arrive soon. I'm sure you'll love my home."

"I doubt that," I reply with a condescending tone. I want him to know I'm upset. Who even does this and gets away with it? People are still dictating my life, and there's nothing I can do to change it.

"You will," he says with a deadly stare. "Whether you want to or not."

"Gee, how nice to be invited into someone's home under the guise of a threat."

"You're not invited as a visitor, Charlotte," he says, placing his glass on the table. "You're my captive."

Finally, he says the words. The actual goddamn truth … that I'm a prisoner of a devilish man with sinister goals.

"I'm glad you admit that you took me against my will. It'll make it easier to explain to the cops once we land," I quip.

A dark smile mars his face. "It's amusing that you think you'll actually have a chance to speak to anyone except me." The tip of his tongue darts out to wet his lips, and for some reason, it has every drop of my attention. "Make no mistake, Charlotte, I won't let anyone come close enough to touch you. You're mine and mine alone for the rest of your life. And if you even dare to try to talk to someone, you're responsible for your father's life and what happens to it."

His dark, gleaming eyes tell me this isn't an empty threat. He means it.

My nostrils flare as I suck in a deep breath. In a fit of rage, I grab my champagne glass and throw the contents all over his nice black suit. "Asshole," I curse under my breath.

"Really, Charlotte? Did you have to do that?" he murmurs, wiping himself down with a napkin. "Don't answer. You'll only make a bigger mess for yourself, and I assure you that's the opposite of what you want." He narrows his eyes at me, and the smile disappears from his face completely. "Because you know you'll be punished for this, don't you?"

The implications of what he said send a chill run down my spine.

"Do you like seeing me in agony?" I ask, biting the inside of my cheeks. "Do you get off on hurting me?"

"Don't ask questions you already know the answer to, Charlotte. It's unbecoming of you, and you know better than to waste my time," he says arrogantly, tucking the napkin into the bin below the table.

"So the answer is yes. What did I ever do to you to deserve this?"

"You father is the cause of your misery, remember?" he

hints as if it's not at all his idea.

"But you were the one who took me, and now his debt is repaid," I say. "So you agreed to all of it."

"Correct ... as long as you remain mine, of course. Otherwise, the debt remains, and he will pay for that with his life," he replies as if murdering my father is not at all a big thing.

"You'd really kill him?" I sneer.

He narrows his eyes at me but doesn't respond. Typical. Talkative when I don't care, and completely silent when I need answers. I take a deep breath and ask my next question. "You have an unhealthy obsession with my family, don't you?"

I don't think this was a random deal. He must've known about my father's financial trouble, and he jumped in like a shark sniffing blood.

"Very smart, princess," he says, cocking his head.

"Stop calling me that," I spit. Constantly belittling me probably makes him feel powerful, bigger than he really is. But nothing he says can bring me down. Nothing. I won't let it happen.

His brow lifts as if he's amused by my outburst. "*What? Spoiled little princess?*"

I make a face. He thinks he knows me? "That's not who I am. At all."

He's wrong. Dead wrong. And I *will* prove it when I escape his grasp and beat him at his own game.

"You don't even know how lucky you are, how lucky

you have been all your life," he hisses. "But you'll learn soon enough." The seat belt sign illuminates above our heads, and he immediately moves into action. "Now buckle up, princess. We're about to land."

SIX

Charlotte

1 Year Ago

After that painful dinner at my father's house, I didn't wanna go home and end the night crying my eyes out while watching Netflix and chugging down a whole bottle of wine, so instead, I got a cab and went out. The city lights have always managed to lift my mood. Besides, I could use a drink, and plenty of places have amazing cocktails.

Not only that, but I heard about a new place up ahead called Dutch Deviants. I've never been there before, but a lot of people are talking about it. It's the place to be, I've heard, so I'm eager to see what's happening.

When the cabbie drops me off, I open my purse and reapply my lipstick before going inside. It looks so luxurious with all the gold shimmer on the tables and walls, and the soft purple mesh hanging throughout the room, making it look like a sultan's throne room. Not a lot of people are dancing; most of them are lounging on one of the many black couches and comfy-looking seats. I guess this place is more for relaxing and less about the loud music, which is a plus to me.

I go to the bar area and check their cocktail menu. The extensive list has a lot of weird combinations, like vodka and lime with a hint of rose petals or apple juice and Turkish fruit mixed with gin.

"I'd go for the Lotus Heaven."

I turn my head and am pleasantly surprised by the familiar blue eyes staring back at me.

"Easton," I mutter. In shock, I stare at his beautiful face, which hasn't changed in years. Still the short, wavy dark hair, chin cleft, and thick, kissable lips. God, did I always mumble like this in front of him?

He reaches for me, and for a second there, I question whether he's going to grab me and kiss me right then. Instead, he grabs the menu and holds it up in front of me, sliding his finger down toward the description of the Lotus Dream.

"Lotus flower and almonds mixed with rum," he says. "An exquisite taste, if I say so myself."

The charming smile that forms on his lips makes my heart flutter. "I can't believe it."

"What? The Lotus flower?"

"No ... well, that too," I stammer, "but more the fact that you're—"

He places a finger on my lips, and says, "No need to explain." He smiles again, this time with an obvious arrogance. "I must say I'm ... pleasantly surprised to find you here."

My cheeks flush, and I lower my eyes. I can't even look at him without turning into a puddle of goo. What's wrong with me? He never used to have this effect on me, right? Or maybe I just denied it.

He flicks his fingers at the bartender, and says, "Lotus Dream. Two. On the house."

My lips part, but I don't know quite what to say, especially when he winks.

"You look stunning," he muses. Grabbing the drinks off the counter, he hands one to me. "There you go."

"Thank you," I say, a bit flabbergasted.

"Go on then," he urges, so I take a sip.

Heavenly. Totally unlike what I expected. "Mmm ..."

An arrogant smirk spreads across his face. "I know, right? It's one of my favorites."

I lick my lips and clutch my glass tight. "But ... why are you ...?"

"Here? Good question. I wasn't planning to visit any of my venues tonight, but then I got bored and decided to have a drink."

I narrow my eyes. "Wait … *your* venues?"

He nods. "We haven't spoken in quite a while, have we?" he muses, then taps my glass with his, and says, "Cheers and enjoy."

And then he walks off into the crowd.

I don't want to be a stalker, but when the only guy who ever captured my interest walks away as though it means nothing, I need to know where he's going. I wanna talk to him. What has he been up to all these years? The last time I saw him was at that restaurant where his father used to work … before my father hired him. My father forced me to ignore him back then, and if I didn't do what he wanted, I'd face punishment. I was too afraid to speak up. But I regret it, and now that I have the chance to apologize, I want to take the opportunity to.

I chase after him through the busy crowd and up a flight of stairs to a giant balcony overlooking the city. He's leaning down on the railing with his arms, staring out into the abyss below while sipping his drink.

When I walk toward the edge, I mutter, "Wow."

"Beautiful, isn't it?" he says as he takes another sip. "It's exactly why I wanted it built here."

"I have to say I am impressed," I say. I never imagined him building a company, let alone something this huge and gorgeous.

He stares into the distance. "Whenever I need to take a breather, I come up here."

"It's a great place to spend time alone," I say, and I lean my back against the balcony while looking at him.

He glances at me over his shoulder, and that one look has me feeling weak to the bone. I don't know what it is about him that makes me feel this way. "I never thought I'd bump into you here."

"Yet here I am," I reply, taking a sip of my drink.

"Strange ... but nice too." He sets my soul on fire with that killer smile. Stepping away from the edge again, he takes another sip of his drink. "So tell me what brought you here."

"Ahh ..." I gaze down at my feet. "My father. You know how he is ..."

"Unfortunately, yes," he says.

"I'm sorry for how he treated you back then," I say, licking my lips. "And I was a bitch for ignoring you."

A lopsided grin spreads on his lips, and he holds up his hand. "Your father was harsh on you."

"Still is," I say, sighing as I put down my drink. "Sorry, TMI, I know."

"You feel choked around him."

"Exactly!" I say. It feels as if he can read my thoughts. "And the worst part is that he wants me to help him, but I don't think I can."

"How?" he asks.

"He wants me to marry some rich stranger so he can save his company ..."

"Hmm ..." He rubs his chin, and mutters, "Interesting."

"Not really. I just shouted at him and ran off. He's probably still fuming." I cross my arms over my chest. "But I don't care."

"Sounds like you do," he jests, making me side-eye him.

"You're still as obnoxious as you were at my father's wedding."

"Have you looked in the mirror recently?" he retorts, making me laugh. He takes the last sip from his glass. "So tell me why you followed me."

"No reason. To apologize for my father and my behavior, I suppose. But that was it."

"Really?" He raises a brow. "Weren't you just a little bit captivated with the idea of me owning all these businesses?" He steps closer. "You think now that you've apologized, I'll forgive you?" I swallow away the lump in my throat. He's so close I can feel his breath on my skin. "It'll take a lot more groveling for me to forget how you treated me."

I'm mortified. "But I just … my father …" I'm frozen to my spot because of his closeness, and I can't even think straight, let alone speak properly.

"Now that I've built up all these businesses and accumulated some wealth, you think I'm suddenly good enough to talk to?" he sneers.

Where does this sudden hostility come from? "I never said you weren't—"

"You ignored me and let your father have his way," he growls. "If you'd stopped him, maybe my father would've …"

His father? What does his father have to do with it? All I know is that his father worked for my father as a chef at one of his restaurants, and then he suddenly didn't anymore, but my father never lets me in on his business.

Easton's nostrils flare, and he takes a deep breath. "Leave. Just go."

I suck on my bottom lip and shake my head. "I'm sorry. I didn't want to be such an asshole, but my father gave me no choice."

He smacks the glass from my hand, and it drops to the floor, shattering into a million pieces.

"GO!" His sudden outburst has me fleeing from the balcony, rushing all the way down the stairs and out of the club.

I don't know what made him turn on me like that. Why, one minute, it's as if he wants to rekindle whatever it is we had, and then the next, he wants to put me to shame.

But it's too late to apologize. I'm not coming back here ever again.

***

EASTON

A few days later

I'd purposely opened my business in several cities around the world and specifically here because I knew this was where her parents lived. I'd looked that up a long time ago. Never did I imagine I'd run into her at one of my clubs, but it made for a good surprise.

Though, I'm not sure I was truly happy to see her. After all, she broke my heart in several ways, and her father is a heartless monster. Those dollar bills that pompous idiot is sniffing right now are dipped in blood.

My blood.

And I will make him pay for what he did.

One way or another, he will beg me for mercy. And I know just the way.

Her disclosure that his company is in trouble and needs financial investors is the perfect entry for me. It's as if she knew I was in my darkest hour and offered her sweet, ripe cherry in return.

I could give her father a loan and make him pay by taking her.

Charlotte Davis. My wife. *My pet.*

A wicked grin spreads across my lips. It's almost too good to be true, but it's the best idea I've ever had. The best idea she's ever given me.

It was so easy to get into her apartment.

Once she ran off, I had her followed, and when I knew where she lived, all I had to do was look under the potted plant for a spare key. Stupid girl ... doesn't she realize that's how dirty men like me get inside her home?

Hearing her breathe softly into her pillow as she sleeps the night away entices me. Her chest rises and falls with each breath she takes, and her eyes flutter in her REM sleep. Is she dreaming of me and our chance encounter? Or is she dreaming of a way to escape the nightmare that encompasses her entire life?

I inch closer, lured in by her magnificent scent. I want to raise the sheets, grab her, and take her away right now.

But I have to hold myself back. It would definitely ruin the plan I have in mind.

So I step back again, each time a little farther, savoring every inch of her as a snapshot that I'll keep in my mind for my own pleasure.

Oh, filthy little bird, with your strawberry lips and fairy-like pink hair ... you will be mine.

Soon.

SEVEN

EASTON

Present

My excitement intensified the moment we landed. Not just because we're back in the country where I live, where I know the people better, and where I feel at home, but also because I couldn't wait to see her face once she realized there was no fucking way she'd ever be able to talk to anyone—not the cops, not any other flyers, and not any personnel. Too bad for her, she still had hopes that'd be the case.

Those hopes got crushed the second my limo met us on the airstrip to pick us up right when we walked off the jet. The look in her eyes was magnificent. The despair grew with time and turned her into a dark, shivering mess. Like a ghost floating through the air, she settled into her seat. I didn't even have to force her. She went inside my mansion without a fight, which was a nice surprise.

It's always incredibly fascinating to watch people disintegrate in front of me. I can't ever get enough. Maybe that makes me a sadistic asshole, but I don't give a damn. I love it. It gets me going, making me want to put my hands all over her and show her who's boss.

She hasn't ever been around an actual man, and that's about to change. I know she can feel it. The air in this car is thick with unspoken words and desire. I can almost taste her submission. It won't be long until she fully commits … I'm sure of it. And then I'll make her my wife.

She might think I'm only in it for the short term, but I want her for the long run. I want her body and soul. And I want her by her own choice. I want her to submit out of her own free will.

I want her spreading her legs, waiting for my finger. I want her on her knees begging for my cock. And I want her to willfully put my ring on her own damn finger, knowing it's forever.

It's not just about owning her. I've already accomplished that by purchasing her from her father in exchange for a simple loan. No, I want her to crumple and admit defeat. She might not realize this now, but she will in due time.

I clear my throat when we drive through the gates of my home, and she shifts in her seat. She seems anxious, sweat drops gleaming on her forehead as she stares out the back window at the closing gates.

She may be scoping her surroundings, trying to find a way out, but there is none. I have plenty of guards to keep her from escaping should she try. Not to mention the fact that my house is locked down 24/7 unless I'm there.

She's going to be a pretty princess in a pretty castle, just like she always dreamed of.

"We're here," I say as the limo stops in front of the door. Seeing my house is refreshing. I'm so glad I moved back to this country. It was my home for so many years, and it never felt right in America. Despite being born there, this is where I belong.

Charlotte sucks in a breath but doesn't say a word. The scowl on her face speaks volumes, though.

I get out of the car and walk to the other side to open her door and hold my hand out courteously. Instead, she gets out without even touching me, passing me on high heels and narrowly missing a puddle. Adventurous girl, that's for sure.

She walks up the steps and inside the door that's already opened for her by one of my butlers. She wanders into the main hall, then looks around without moving an inch.

I place a hand on her shoulder. Her muscles tense, and a grin spreads on my lips in response.

"Do you like it here?" I ask.

She licks her lips briefly, and says, "When will you let me go?"

This again?

"Never," I reply, narrowing my eyes. "Why do you keep asking?"

She looks me straight in the eyes as she answers. "I won't ever stop asking."

My throat tightens, and I swallow in response. I didn't expect her to say that. She's not dumb; she already knows the answer. The only reason she will ask me again and again ... is to confront me with my choice. To make me see the devil I've become.

But I don't care. I came to that same conclusion long ago when I decided to go through with this.

"When did you turn into such a monster?" she asks.

The question is like a stab to the heart with a butcher's knife. As if she doesn't know the answer to that full well ... that she's the reason I am the way I am today. Simple cause and effect, and her denying me even a simple smile set into motion a chain of events that can't ever be undone.

"The moment you ignored me. You listened to *him* instead of your heart. That was enough for me," I growl.

Her parted lips close.

The doors close behind us, leaving a deafening silence in their wake.

"You know how violent my father is. You saw it with your own eyes," she says, pain stinging her voice. "I had no choice but to ignore you."

"You could've stood your ground. You know as well as I do this is your fault. All of this is your doing."

"No, you're lying to yourself. And you let yourself become a monster," she hisses.

"Your father hated my guts, and you let him control you," I retort.

"He tries to control everyone," she says. "That doesn't make this okay. Why do you want to ruin us so badly?"

"I will do everything I can to destroy the Davis name," I growl. "Because of *your* father, my father is now dead."

"What?" Her eyes widen. "Your father?" She shakes her head. "No, that's not possible. My father wouldn't murder—"

My blood boils. "Your father worked mine to death."

"That wasn't his—"

"Yes, it was!" Anger seeps through my veins, and I explode. "Your father *wanted* my father to succumb to the stress as payback for me trying to get close to you. Because of *you* ... *my* father is dead."

***

1 Year Ago

After the falling out I had at the restaurant with that pompous asshole Davis, I didn't want to stand between my father and his biggest job ever. I wanted him to succeed, even if it was without me, so I stopped working for him and settled on getting my own shit sorted.

I opened my own high-end club for singles, and after

gathering some investors, I managed to open a couple more over the years. I even paid all of them off within no time. I never expected my business would skyrocket this fast, but I guess people enjoy the unique cocktails we serve and the luxurious atmosphere at the locations.

The more clubs I open all around the world, the more the opportunity arises to spend and earn big money, which is what I wanted all along ... To grow my business into an empire and outsmart that son of a bitch Davis. One day, I will be richer than he is, and then I'll buy out all of his businesses and make him pay. I'll ruin him until he has nothing left to spit on. And then we'll see who has the last laugh.

But first, it's time to see how my father's doing. I haven't seen him in a month, and he's been quiet during our phone conversations lately, so I decided to drop by his house tonight.

The only thing he told me was that Davis put so much pressure on him to perform that he wasn't even allowed to stay home sick. I hate that prick like nobody else, but my father never listened to him when I told him he needed to quit while he still could. Now, Davis holds his paycheck over his head ... and he works like a goddamn hostage.

The thought makes my fists clench as I ring the doorbell a couple of times.

No one comes to the door. "Father?" I bang on the wood a couple of times but still no answer. "Father?" He's always home at this hour. I don't wanna go straight to my last resort, but it seems I have no choice.

My father gave me a spare key to his apartment a few months back in case I needed to drop by for something like supplies or to help him out sometimes. Guess now's the time to use it.

I fish the key from my pocket and jam it into the keyhole, twisting it until the door unlocks. I open it wide and call out for my father again.

But as I step inside and take a look around, I freeze, and the key drops from my hand. He's lying on the floor completely lifeless.

"Father!" I rush toward him and go down to my knees in front of his body, shaking him vigorously. I place my index finger against his neck and check for a pulse. Nothing.

Placing my hands on top of his chest, I immediately start compressions. After countless times, I blow air into his mouth while holding his nose. But nothing I do seems to get him to breathe again.

I don't know how long I continue or how much time passes before I call an ambulance. Before they tell me that I did my best, but that there is no saving him. He died from a heart attack caused by too much stress. He'd been working so hard lately, and it'd been the death of him.

In the hospital waiting room, my hands feel cold and my heart empty, devoid of any emotion. All I can do is stare into oblivion as I realize my father's been taken away from me.

Too soon.

EIGHT

EASTON

Present

"No ..." She keeps shaking her head.

"You can believe whatever you want, Charlotte, but it's the truth."

"I don't believe it," she hisses. "You can't blame that on me."

"Doesn't matter what you think or believe. You're the reason your father worked mine to death. And now I will make *you* pay ... and then your father." A wicked grin spreads on my lips. "All that matters is that you're here in my home now, and you will abide by my wishes like a good fucking girl."

"Fuck. You," she spits, and she runs toward the doors, banging on them hard. "Let me out! Let me out, please!"

Approaching her from behind, I grab her shoulders when she doesn't stop and swiftly spin her on her heels and shove her against the doors.

"*No one* is going to let you out. Do you hear me? *No one*. No one will listen to you. No one ... except me." Her chest rises with each breath, and beads of sweat glisten on her exposed skin right above her top. "You're ... a vixen. You think you can spin me around your finger, but I won't dance to your tune." I tip her chin up with my index finger and force her to look at me. "Not anymore, Charlotte. You're mine now, and the only one who's going to dance is you."

She grinds her teeth. "Over my dead body."

We face off for a few seconds, staring each other down. I want her to feel intimidated, but I won't force myself on her. I want her to do it on her own terms so she'll remember the moment forever.

For now, I back off and let her stomp up the stairs.

"Your room's on the left!" I yell after her.

But she's already found it and slammed the door shut.

Such a feisty girl ... I'll definitely have my hands full.

***

Charlotte

My bedding was velvety black linen. Lined with gold, the walls surround me like a beautiful cage for a trapped princess. The burgundy red drapes match the color of my father's blood if I ever were to escape. Staring at the windows, I see they're locked with a key I don't have access to. I wonder where he keeps it or if I should even go look for it.

I'm plagued by thoughts of fleeing, but then I see my father's dead eyes staring right back at me, and I stop. I can't. Besides, I don't know anyone in this country. I wouldn't know where to run if I even had the chance.

I sit down on the bed and stare ahead at the boudoir at the other end of the room. The person in the mirror gazes back at me, but I don't recognize her. All I see are two broken eyes filled with tears.

But I don't want to cry.

I don't want to see the girl in the mirror, who had her whole life ahead of her, stolen away from her world just to be put into a beautiful prison.

Instead, I walk toward the potted plant next to the boudoir, and I pick it up and chuck it at the mirror. A loud, visceral shriek emanates from my lungs. Even though it's only a fraction of the pain I feel, I had to get it out of my system. Nothing I do will still this rage in my veins.

I want to scream and pound on the door until my fists bleed, scratch the wood until the splinters bury underneath my nails, until nothing's left but emptiness.

Just like me.

I feel hollow inside. As though I've been stripped of all that it means to be alive. As if I'm imprisoned with my worst enemy.

I caused this. Easton fell for me, and my father hated him for it. And because of my inability to stand up to my father, he ran all over Easton and his family ... and it killed his father.

I made Easton hate me, made him want me so badly he'd trick my father into giving him me just for revenge. It's stupid I ever thought and felt anything good for this man, and that I ever listened to my father and came to that diner.

My mind is plagued with what-ifs and guilt, and it's consuming me.

A sudden knock on the door pulls me from my anguish.

"Excuse me. Mr. Van Buren requires you downstairs for dinner," a voice speaks out.

I don't respond. I don't even know what to say to that ... person. Whoever it is. Do they honestly expect me to come out and *eat* with that monster? No. I'd rather starve than sit next to him and pretend everything's fine when it's not.

"Will you come and eat dinner with him?" the voice asks

again.

"No," I growl back. "Leave me alone."

Footsteps fade away, so I guess they've gone downstairs. I wonder who it was ... and who'd ever choose to work for such an asshole. Just like the driver who brought us to the restaurant and picked us up from the airstrip, or the pilot who flew the airplane, or any of the other people who work for him. Do they do it willingly, or are they forced into it by debt as well?

It wouldn't surprise me. He's such an asshole ... ugh, I can't believe I ever liked this guy. That I ever felt anything but hostility toward him is mind-blowing. At my father's wedding, he was such a nice young guy. Did he change that drastically just from me ignoring him that one time? That can't possibly be it; no way did I have that much effect on someone's personality. Right? But he said it did.

I sigh and lie down on the bed, staring at the ceiling. Guess there's nothing else to do but sit around and wait ... Maybe I'll go on the prowl when things go quiet and everyone's gone to bed. At least then I won't have to talk to *him*.

***

A few hours later, I pry open the door and softly tread down the stairs. It's dark all around me as the sun has already set, and no one seems to be around. I waited long enough to make sure everyone would've gone to bed or be at home right now. I don't know whether his workers sleep in his mansion, but I didn't wanna risk running into any of them.

My growling stomach reminds me I haven't eaten in a while, so I go straight to the kitchen on the left of the stairs to see if I can find something. It's huge with marble tiles everywhere, oak walls and cabinets on the sides, and a huge cooking island complete with expensive pottery and pans hanging from a ceiling rack. If I wasn't a prisoner here, I'd say the place was like a dream. Except this is more like a worst-nightmare scenario.

Still, I'm not gonna sit around and do nothing while I'm hungry as hell. There must be something in the fridge that I can eat. A delish chocolate cake stares right back at me the moment I open the door, and my mouth waters. No one will notice if I take a piece, right? It's already been cut anyway.

I reach inside the fridge and take out the cake, placing it on the gray marble counter before searching the drawers for a knife. However, I find that all of them are locked.

"Looking for this?"

The sudden sound of his voice has me jolting up and down and holding in a squeal.

Easton holds up a sharp knife. I don't know where he got it ... or how he even discovered me here in the first place. I immediately check my surroundings; the walls, the door, everything because there *must* be a camera, right? How else would he have known where I was?

I back away, bumping into the counter with my hips as he approaches me. The sharp blade in his hand gleams, and I swallow hard as Easton comes close with it.

"Hungry, huh?" he asks. Cocking his head, he glances at the cake next to me.

I don't say a word. I don't want to give him more ammo.

Even though, according to him, I'm responsible for his pain and suffering ... I refuse to let it get to me.

"Here, let me help you," Easton says, tightening the rope around his robe before leaning in to the cake. He takes a whiff, purposely watching me as my mouth waters and my lips part. God, I wish I could have a taste, but I don't wanna give him that pleasure.

"You can have a bite ..." he muses, sticking the knife inside and cutting a piece in a very violent manner. He grabs a plate and scoots the cake onto it, bringing it up to my face.

"Smells so good, doesn't it?" he asks, a wicked smile forming on his face. "But wait ..."

Right as I lean toward the plate, he pulls it away again and fishes a key from the pocket in his bathrobe. With it, he opens a drawer beside me and takes out a fork, then immediately locks it again. Then he picks up the plate and takes off a piece of cake with the fork, holding it in front of my mouth.

"Open up," he muses, sliding it across my lips.

But the possessive look in his eyes tells me this is more than satiating my hunger. This is about power, a game of cat and mouse, so I keep my mouth shut and stare straight ahead. His pitch-black eyes show no mercy.

"Open your mouth, Charlotte," he says, this time with a more domineering voice. The way he holds the fork near my mouth, brushing it along my lips feels as if he's trying to kiss me with an object.

I don't know if denying him is the smart thing to do here because I don't want to anger him. What if he lashes out? Then again, I don't want him to believe I'll become a meek little lamb. But what harm can a little cake do?

My grumbling stomach has decided for me, so I open my mouth. He slides the fork inside, and his gaze follows my lips as they close, taking the cake in my mouth. His eyes bore into me as I chew on the delicious piece and swallow it down. A satisfying groan leaves his mouth.

I feel naked. Watched. Used.

As if he only did this because it reminded him of something far dirtier.

The cake suddenly doesn't taste as good anymore.

He scoops another piece with the fork and attempts to push it inside my mouth too, but I turn my head away.

"C'mon now ..." he murmurs. "Have another bite. You love it. I can tell."

"No," I say. "I want to do it myself."

"You eat *when* I tell you to eat, and you eat how *I want* you to eat," he replies.

I refuse without words. He knows what I think. One look is enough.

Suddenly, he throws the plate on the floor, shattering it and covering the tiles with chocolate.

"Then stay hungry! I don't fucking care," he growls, pointing at the door. "Go! Go to your fucking room and don't come out until I say so."

I stay put, grasping the marble countertop and curling my toes while expecting his blowback. We already passed the stage of him becoming enraged, so now all I can do is make a choice; either run like a weakling or face the threat head on.

"I'm not a robot," I reply with as much grace as I can muster. I won't sink to his level.

"No, you are my hostage," he says, his tongue dipping out to lick the top of his lips as if he's contemplating what that means. Like the word hostage automatically means I'm supposed to do anything he wants. But that's just it. Even as a hostage, I still have my own autonomy. I can still choose not to think or feel whatever he wants me to. He can own my body ... but not my heart or soul.

The chilling silence between us speaks volumes. It tells me he knows this same thing.

His nostrils flare, and he averts his eyes, rubbing his lips together. He closes his eyes completely as he turns away from me and rubs his forehead with the palm of his hand.

"Get out," he says, but his much softer voice confuses me.

Where's the anger? Debris litters the whole kitchen, and he's standing there with slumped shoulders as if nothing ever happened. As though he's … ashamed.

"Leave me," he says, still pointing toward the door as he clicks some kind of button hanging on the wall near the stove. "Someone will escort you to your room."

Within a minute, someone has arrived. A curly-haired male employee, from the looks of it, complete with outfit. As if they don't ever sleep.

He gestures me to follow him, so I do. I don't want to give Easton the satisfaction of winning this fight, but I need to remove myself from this situation before it gets out of hand.

I can tell he had to stop himself from going any further … As if he was dying to grab me and do something to me. But the way he stared at me while I ate that piece of cake, with such a beastly glare, made me feel … powerless. Like he was going to fuck me right there and then on the kitchen countertop.

My heart palpitates, and I clench my legs together as I follow the man up the stairs. I can't stop thinking about how Easton literally tried to feed me. At first, I thought he was only trying to get to me, to make me feel like a child, but he was so transfixed on my lips that I felt naked. And I don't like that feeling at all.

Shivers run up and down my spine as we arrive at my door, and the employee kindly opens the door as if it's some kind of service to me and not at all as an accomplice to his employer's schemes.

"Do you work for him?" I ask as I walk inside and turn

around to face him.

"Yes, ma'am," he says as he attempts to close the door.

I put my foot out to stop the door. "What's your name?" I ask before I lose the chance.

"You can call me Nick, ma'am," he replies.

"And you agree with all this?" I ask. "You know I'm a prisoner here, right?"

"Ma'am …" He sighs. "We're not allowed to speak with you about this."

"So you know yet you choose to do nothing?" I say, cocking my head as he continues to try to close the door on me.

"Good night." He manages to push my foot back inside and immediately shuts the door, locking me inside.

Fuck.

I punch the door several times. "You can't keep me in here!"

But no one replies to my calls. No matter how many times I bang, and say, "Let me out!"

It all falls on deaf ears. But I know Easton can hear me.

I know because he's been watching me all this time. He knows where I am whenever I leave this room. Hell, I wouldn't be surprised if he was watching me right now. He just chooses not to respond to my cries. Like a true cruel man keeping a girl hostage.

After a while, I turn around and fall onto the bed facedown. Not wanting to face reality, I curl up into the fetal position and close my eyes, wishing the tears away.

NINE

EASTON

One hiccup. Two hiccups. A sniff.

With my ear pressed against her door, I can hear every sound, every breath.

I can't stop biting my lip as I listen, wondering what she's doing right now. Something muffles her cries, a pillow perhaps. I imagine her hugging it tight as she curls up on my guest bed ... *her* bed. In *her* room. The room I gave her as a prison to stay in.

I shouldn't be here.

But I can't stay away either. Wherever she is, I've always wanted to follow. It's what drove me to her in the first place, what made me take her away from her father.

She's right. I'm a cruel monster who only cares about his own desires. But a part of me, somewhere deep inside, wishes for something else too. Something ... better. Something real.

But we can't have that. We never could and never will.

Not when she's my hostage, someone I keep in a soft and velvety cage for my selfish needs.

My hand lingers on the wood, nails digging in as my heart sinks into my shoes. I'm fighting the urge to unlock the door and go inside.

I have no place in her room. Not after taunting her to the brink of despair. Did I go too far? The knife and fork were only a game—a way to toy with her emotions—but the sight of her obeying me filled me with such power that it consumed me and made me lash out. I wanted her to eat that cake until she was full and then sink to her knees and take my cock as a second dessert.

But that was a filthy dream of mine. Nothing more.

I should've known my fantasies would interfere with my ability to reason. I couldn't keep my cool and made her face the rage inside me. Of course, she's upset.

I close my eyes and let out a sigh. I don't want to be this mean. I want to make her happy.

But I want her to suffer too, and those wishes clash like hell. I want her to know what it did to me when she chose to deny me and chose her goddamn father over me. That fucking arrogant son of a bitch who didn't even love her ... who ruined her for me.

Who worked my father to death ... literally.

Taking in a deep breath, I lean away from the door and stare at it for a few seconds. Then I turn around and walk away. But there will come a time when I won't be able to keep that door locked. When I won't stop myself from touching her ... from kissing her. And that day will be here sooner than she thinks.

***

When morning comes, I instruct Nick to unlock her door and tell her to dress so we can eat breakfast. It takes her a while to come down—two hours, to be precise—and I don't know why she needed that much time. The hunger must've gotten a bit too much for her to cope with, which I assumed would be the case. It doesn't take long for a person to break when it comes to food. Just like water and sleep, it's essential for a person to survive ... and also the perfect tool for getting someone to do your bidding.

And what I want right now is for her to eat with me at this big table that is otherwise pretty empty without her. I've looked forward to this moment for ages.

When she enters the room in her floaty white gown that I had custom tailored to her size, it feels as though the entire room suddenly lights on fire. Her beautiful eyes blaze as she glares at me.

I know she hasn't forgiven me yet, but that's okay because I don't expect her to. I do expect her to behave in an orderly fashion, though. As long as she obeys my rules, everyone will be happy and remain alive. Simple.

"Sit," I say, pointing at the chair next to me. There's plenty of space for her to sit, but I've asked them to set the table to ensure we can look each other in the eyes.

She observes the table, standing frozen in place before walking toward the other end of it and sitting as far away from me as possible. The deadly stare she gives me sets my body ablaze. Does she not realize it only makes the urge to grab her and fuck her right here on this table stronger?

All I want is her, and all she wants is to get away from me. How fitting.

A tepid smile forms on my lips as I clear my throat, and say to Nick, "Please bring Miss Davis her plate and cutlery. We wouldn't want her to eat with her hands, now would we?"

She gives me a faux smile accompanied by eyes reduced to mere slits. I honestly imagine she's shooting venom at me at this point, but I don't mind. I know she's upset, and she has every right to be, but that won't change the fact she's mine. I still won't let her go, no matter how hard she tries to pretend she's going to fight me on this.

Soon she'll give in ... and then I'll ravish her bit by bit.

When Nick's done setting the table, the food comes in, and her eyes immediately hone in on the cream-filled bagel I bought early this morning from an American baker in Amsterdam just for her. I know she likes these things, like cranberry juice, coffee without sugar or milk, and a fried egg on toast, sunny side up. All of which are stacked onto a plate and brought to her side of the table right now.

She sure loves pure tastes with no dilution and nothing from a can or a box. Everything has to be fresh with Miss Princess. Her eyes widen at the sight of all that delicious food. Her mouth must be salivating by now. I don't even have to guess … I know because I took extensive notes on all her favorites courtesy of her father's staff … and my own personal research, of course.

I clear my throat, and say, "If you eat your breakfast without protesting, I'll overlook the fact you refused to sit next to me."

She snorts and looks away, shaking her head, but she doesn't respond. Typical for her, but I know she's thinking a myriad of things. She's just afraid to say them out loud.

I pick up my bagel and take a bite, but the more I swallow, the less she seems interested in her food.

"Go on. Eat."

"No," she says, folding her arms.

I'm offering her an olive branch right now, and she throws it right back in my face.

"Charlotte, are we going to play this game again?" I raise a brow at her, challenging her attempt to defy me once again. "Please don't try. You know it'll only end in heartbreak."

"You mean pain," she replies. "*My* pain."

I wish her words didn't cut into me the same way I'm slicing through the butter right now, but they do. I do desperately want to hurt her, but not in the way she thinks.

I don't want her to feel the pain that I felt. I want her to feel the pain that makes you squirm, that makes your throat jam and takes your breath away. Not the kind where your heart is ripped out of your chest, thrown on the ground, and stomped on. Because that's what I felt when she didn't even acknowledge my existence in front of her father. Nor does she know the kind of pain you feel when you find your own father lying on the floor dead.

"You don't know what pain is," I growl back, angered by the memory.

She narrows her eyes. "Like you do."

I stab the butter knife into the butter like a butcher's knife into meat. "You don't fucking know what I've been through, so don't even try."

"Really? Tell me then. Tell me how hard the world has been to you," she jests, trying to get under my skin. It won't work. I won't let it.

"Eat. Your. Breakfast," I say with a low, commanding voice. Then I proceed to eat my bagel and take a sip of my coffee.

"Only if you tell me why. Why all of this 'pretending' to be happy? Why do you even care? You already have me. What more could you want?"

I look up from my food, narrowing my eyes at her as I answer. "Your heart and soul ... and I won't stop until they belong to me."

"Then you'll die trying," she says, picking up her bagel

and taking a defiant bite. She can even turn food into an object of aggression. I don't know how she does it, but she makes me want to dig my nails into my skin until I bleed.

"You say that now, but you'll warm up to me eventually," I say. Her tongue dips out to lick the spread from her lips, and I wish that was my tongue instead. Fuck.

"Why do you think that?" she asks, taking another bite.

"Because I charmed you once …" An arrogant smile curls my lips. "I can do it again."

"Before I knew what a manipulative bastard you were, you mean," she retorts.

"You're angry because I do everything in my power to get what I want," I say, and I put my coffee down. "Make no mistake, Charlotte. I may look like a gentleman, but I'm far from it. My only interest from the start has been to destroy your father's business and take you as a prize."

"I'm not a fucking object," she hisses.

There she goes again with that dirty mouth of hers, but I like it. "You should swear more often. It takes the edge off things," I taunt.

"Stop. Stop playing these games," she spews.

"No. I like it when you're uncomfortable," I reply, cocking my head. "Gets me off."

She growls out loud and then throws her bagel onto her plate. Leaning back in her chair, she crosses her arms across her chest with a scowl on her face. She reminds me of a child who's not getting her way, but that's something we can work on. After all, we have all the time in the world.

"So you planned this all along?" she mutters. "Tell me how."

Does she really want to know? I can tell her, but it'll only make her hate me more. Then again, maybe she'll finally take me seriously and start listening. "I bought the last of your father's stock and then sold it dirt cheap to make the markets plummet."

She grabs the napkin to dab her lips, but she can't help but scrunch it up in her hand as I talk.

"A few phone calls were all it took to make the other shareholders start selling … and for the price to drop like a stone in the water. It didn't take long for the company to go bust and for his wife to abandon him and take whatever he had left. Poor fucker. I should feel sorry for him, shouldn't I? But I'm glad he took my loan afterward. I was the only one who would offer him one after his business went to shit, of course." I chuckle and take the last bite of my bagel, but Charlotte doesn't seem remotely amused. What a surprise.

"So it was you?" she hisses, barely able to control herself. I wonder what she's going to do as she clenches the napkin in her hand. Will she try to throw her knife at me? Or will she dig her claws into my skin to make it personal?

"You ruined him and his company and then took me too just for fun …" she murmurs.

I brace myself for the ensuing fight. I wait and wait … except nothing happens.

Instead, she begins to sniff, her eyes turning red and

puffy, and then a single tear rolls down her cheeks. Beautifully broken is how she looks ... but still fierce like a lion willing to fight its way out of the cage. And she stands proudly, gives me one fixated glare, and stampedes out the door, leaving me simmering alone. Just as only a true queen would.

TEN

Charlotte

Small specks of snow flutter against the window of my room, turning from ice to water, and then fading away. Just as I am while I'm standing here in this room wearing only a bra and panties as I'm being measured.

The woman taking my size works meticulously without saying a word. She doesn't even look me in the eyes as she puts her hands on my waist and bust. Jill, I think. When she told me her name, it didn't properly register, just like all the other things she's said so far after coming into my room with two racks filled with wedding dresses.

When people talk about an out-of-body experience, I guess this is it because it's as though I'm not even here.

All I can think of is how cold it must be outside, and how much I miss feeling the snowflakes fall onto my skin. I wonder if I'll ever go outside again or if he'll even let me.

My heart is full of melancholy, the kind where you feel like crying but all your tears have dried up. My stare is a blank and unemotional one. I'm fading out of this existence, losing myself in the moment as I'm being pushed around like a puppet on a string.

Jill talks to me, but I'm not listening. My mind is outside … where the people are. They're enjoying the weather with smiles on their faces and playing in the snow with their kids, not even aware of the fact someone's locked up in here. I don't know where I am or if I'll ever get out. I pray people won't forget I exist.

"Miss, can you step aside, please?" Jill asks.

She's so nice, unlike him. It's the first time we've met, but she looks like a person who cares about people, judging from the look she gives me whenever she spins around me and comes face to face with my disinterested gaze. A simple smile is all it takes to make me feel warm in a place that's cold to the bone.

My feet hover aside, and as they do, she places a hoop and a skirt underneath me and pulls it up to my waist, strapping it tight. Then comes the bustier and finally the dress. The ensemble doesn't fit me at all, but with a few pins, she manages to make it wearable for now.

"It'll have to do. It's only a test run," she says, huffing and puffing as she comes to her feet. "What do you think?"

I look down at the dress surrounding my body, the pearly white fabric soft and velvety against my skin, prickling a little when I move my hands. I can't believe I'm wearing this, and that this would be the dress I wear when he marries me.

A shiver runs up and down my spine as Jill nudges me toward the new mirror that Easton had installed. "Go on, have a look."

I hesitate but then step toward the mirror in front of the boudoir anyway, and with a big smile, Jill pushes it aside to create more room for me to strut. Even though I don't want to, I still go to the mirror, and I'm frozen in place. I don't recognize the girl glaring right back at me. She's barely there, and her hands begin to shake vigorously.

"That's not me," I mutter, staring at my puckered red lips, wondering when she put the lipstick on. I can't remember; that's how out of it I am.

"Of course, that's you," Jill says, chuckling as she pats down the dress a little. "You look gorgeous!"

I feel sick. So sick that I immediately run into the bathroom and throw up in the toilet.

Jill comes to help me, holding my hair back along with the dress. "Oh dear," she mumbles, handing me a towel to wipe my mouth. "Are you okay?"

I shake my head as she gets up and fills a cup with water, then gives it to me. "Here, have some water. It'll help wash the taste away."

"Thanks," I mutter, unsure of what to say.

"Are you sure you're okay? You seem so distant," she asks. "Should I call Mr. Van Buren?"

"No, please don't," I interject, immediately getting off the floor. "I'm fine."

She frowns. "You … aren't pregnant, right?"

"What?" My eyes widen. "No. God no. Of course not."

"I wanted to make sure. I don't want to put heavy dresses and tight corsets on you if there's a tiny baby growing inside you." She laughs it off again. "Not to mention, a pregnant girl needs to eat, and you look as thin as a twig."

Gee, thanks for the compliment, I guess.

"I'm not pregnant, don't worry," I say, and I turn my head.

"Well, if you are, do let me know." She places a hand on my shoulder. "I'm always here to help you out."

This woman is actively helping Easton achieve his lifelong goal of tricking me into becoming his wife, and he's succeeding too. I don't understand why anyone helps him, why they even work for him. Who would do this to another human being?

I look her straight in the eyes, and say, "Can you help me then? I don't want to marry Easton."

She cocks her head, her smile disappearing as she cups my face, and says, "Oh, honey, you'll be fine with him. I know you will."

I grab her arms and hold them tight. "I'm being held against my will. Don't you see?" I say in a moment of clarity. She's my only connection to the real world right now. The last lifeline to grab and hold on to for dear life. "Please, you have to help me."

She licks her lips and sighs. "Sweetie … ugh, I wish I could, but I can't. Easton means the best even though he may seem like a giant asshole sometimes."

"He took me as a replacement for a debt my father owed," I reply, fighting the tears. "Please. Help me."

She sucks on her bottom lip. "I'm sorry, honey, but I can't. I wanna help you. I really do."

"Why can't you? Tell me why," I say, almost wanting to shake her. "You have a key, right? He lets you in and out of the house."

"Yes, but I can't use it to let you out," she says, averting her eyes. "That would mean betraying him."

My hands release her arms, my body instantly reverting to a defensive stance as I realize where this is going.

"I can't … I'm sorry. I owe him too much," she says.

Her words mean nothing to me. I should've known she admires him.

"So you won't help me," I murmur, backing away. Of course, she won't. I should've known the minute she didn't speak the language of the people here but regular English. *He* brought her here, probably all the way from America so she could work for him personally without having anything to fall back on.

There's a soft smile on her face. "Oh, honey, please don't say that," she says. "Of course, I'll help. I'll help get you dressed for your big day."

"That's not—"

"I can get you whatever you need. Books, magazines, chocolates, tampons. Whatever you want. Just use the pager he's given you," she interrupts.

"Pager?" I frown.

"Yeah. You haven't seen it?" She turns around and walks toward the boudoir, opening the drawer and pulling out an old pager. "Here. Just page me at 30151, and I'll be right up!"

She stuffs the pager into my hand as if it's some sort of gift. But all it is, is a representation of my captivity. A digital device that does nothing but receive and send messages to the few people he wants me to be able to contact. The only device I'll probably ever get to see again that specifically makes it impossible to contact friends or family. Just as planned.

"Um … thanks," I mutter. I don't know what to say. She's smiling at me in a way that elicits a response. As if I should be happy too.

I'm as far from happy as anyone could ever be, though I won't show that to her. She's his assistant, and someone who adores him. She'd never go against him, no matter how hard I'd try to convince her. I guess that's the power of persuasion. *His* power, which he knows he holds over both of us. It was futile to even try to find help.

"Well, just walk in the dress and enjoy it a little. I'll come back later to try on the others, okay? You're free to pick a few you wanna try out too!" She winks and then leaves the room. I sink to the floor, drowning in my wedding gown as the tears of misery flow down my cheeks.

***

EASTON

My tailor is taking my measurements right now, but I'm too antsy for him to finish. I wish I could snap my fingers and have my navy suit ready to go. But unfortunately, that's not how the world works most of the time.

Just like with women, you have to be patient. Only then will they open up and allow you to enter their domain. That goes for Charlotte too. She's been nothing but difficult ever since she arrived, but that's understandable, considering the circumstances. It's not every day that you get ripped from your daily life and put into a mansion to play wifey for a rich bastard.

She's lucky she had the chance, to be honest. Plenty of girls would die to become mine.

But I want none of them. She's the one for me.

I knew it when I first saw her at her father's wedding, and I knew it when she ignored me at her father's restaurant years later. The more she pushes back, the more I want to pull and tug until she's right where she belongs ... in my arms.

She may be playing hard to get right now, but I *will* make her submit. One way or another, I will be the one to pop her cherry.

God, I can't fucking wait to get my hands on her and shove my dick inside that tight, wet virgin pussy. Her father told me she was untouched, and that better be the truth because I won't settle for anything less. I've dreamed too long, fought too hard for the privilege to let anyone else take it. She won't slip through my fingers; not this time. No, she'll stay right there in her room and wait like the pretty little princess she is until the time arrives, and I come to get her.

On the day when I will fucking make her my wife.

A sudden scream for my name has me up in arms, walking out the door, half-dressed.

Charlotte's in trouble.

ELEVEN

Charlotte

A few minutes earlier

Being alone in a room is the worst thing in the world.

A million wedding dresses surround me. None of them I want to wear, but all of them seem to stare right back at me as I turn and turn, trying to make sense of this all. Even though Jill said I should pick one, I don't want to. Anything but that. I want to scream and shout off the rooftops, but I can't get out of this room to even try. There's no way out ... no way to release this pent-up anger I have left inside me.

Rage boils to the surface, and I run my fingers through

my hair, trying to stop myself from going insane. But I can't. It's too late. Before I know it, I've already reached into the drawers and ripped everything out; clothes, underwear, shoes, belts.

Something shimmery and pointy catches my eye, and I grab a diamond buckle and rip it off the belt. Without thought or reason, I rip it through the dresses, one by one, leaving none of them unscathed. Not even the one I'm wearing.

After I'm done, I scream so loud my lungs feel like they're about to burst. That needed to be let out, and now I feel much better. I sink down onto the bed and breathe in and out slowly. I'm honestly trying not to lose my mind … but I guess it's already too late for that.

Sudden footsteps stomping up the stairs have me clenching the buckle tight, ready to attack. However, the face that appears calms me down immediately. Jill. She's still here?

"Miss, I heard some … oh, my God!" She immediately rushes to the dresses, grabbing each and every one of them right where I ripped the holes through. She plucks out the unusable pieces and holds them up closer as if she can't believe her eyes.

"Did you do this?" she mutters. She clutches the dresses as if they're her babies.

"I …" I can't even answer through the guilt eating away at me. How can I when she's looking at me with such pain in her eyes as though she made these dresses by hand? She didn't, right? I hope to God these weren't hers. I don't want to do this to her. I didn't want to do this to anyone … But I don't wanna be forced to marry a guy I despise either.

"These dresses were beautiful," she mumbles. "Gorgeous. And you wrecked them."

"I'm sorry. I shouldn't have, but I couldn't stop either," I try to explain, but I know she won't understand. How could she when she chooses his happiness over my freedom?

Suddenly, Easton bursts through the door, wearing only a pair of navy pants. He's completely naked from the waist up … completely ripped from V-line all the way up to his muscular chest, and my eyes can't stop ogling him. Shit.

His eyes scour the dresses, his nostrils flaring as he witnesses the destruction I caused. He goes over each and every destroyed part until his smoldering eyes land on me. I clench my legs together as he steps farther into the room, his shoulders rising and falling hard with each breath.

"Jill. Leave us."

She nods and leaves the room, closing the door on her way out.

Now it's just the monster and me alone in the room. He stalks closer, his tongue dipping out to lick his bottom lip as though he's preparing for the words to pour out. I'd be lying if I said I wasn't feeling overpowered by his menacing presence as he towers over me, tilting his head as he looks down upon me. His penetrating stare makes me feel naked.

Will it always feel like this? If so, I'll have one heck of a time adjusting to the sight of him, especially if I continue to let a man's chiseled, half-naked body distract me.

I swallow away the lump in my throat as he puts his hands against his waist.

Oh, boy. This is gonna get rough.

***

EASTON

"Did you do this?" I ask, pointing at the dresses littering the floor ... or what's left of them. When she screamed, I thought she'd hurt herself, not ruined the dresses she was supposed to try on. An entire fortune ripped apart as if it means nothing to her.

She averts her eyes, refusing to even look at me. She doesn't want to give me the satisfaction of her guilt. And I'm sure that if she did look at me, she'd turn into a meek little lamb. I know she desires me, and whether she ignores the sensations of her body is irrelevant. Her eyes already betrayed her the moment I set foot into her room.

But that does not change the fact that she acted out like the little princess she is.

I grasp her chin and force her to look me in the eyes. "Tell me why."

"You know damn well why," she hisses through gritted

teeth, trying her best not to look at my bare chest. How amusing. I guess it's hard to avoid looking at something you really wanna look at. Just like it's hard not to ruin someone else's hard work.

"Those were expensive dresses you were supposed to try on, not make a collage out of them."

She snorts. "You think that's what I was doing?"

I tighten my grip on her chin to keep her from turning her head. "You're avoiding the inevitable, Charlotte." A smile forms on my lips as her fear grows when I bend over to get on her eye level. "You *will* be my wife, whether you like it or not, and you *will* wear whatever I tell you to wear."

"There are no dresses left. What are you gonna do?" she taunts.

"You think this will get you out of the agreement?" I retort, shaking my head slightly.

I put my hands beside her on the bed, and she leans backward just to avoid confrontation.

"Let me be straight with you. I don't care if I have to drag you to the altar in your bra and panties. I'll fucking put a ring on your finger in front of your family while you are naked if I have to," I growl, leaning so close I could press her down on the mattress and force myself on her. But I'm not gonna do that. I just want her to think I could. She needs to feel the threat and remember it, so she won't ever pull this shit again to try to get her way.

"Make no mistake, princess ..." I whisper as I take a strand of her hair and curl it around my finger. "You are mine, and you will be my wife, with or without a dress. And we'll have plenty of time to enjoy everything that comes with being a husband and wife ... including having you strut around my house completely naked."

Just the thought has me riled up enough to make my cock hard against my pants, and when I lean away, standing tall and proud, her eyes follow down toward my rock-hard length. The way she swallows right after is enough for me.

First, I'll take her hand. Then I'll take her pussy.

"Now ... apologize to me and Jill and promise you won't do silly things like this again. Maybe then I'll let you have dinner tonight."

She grimaces and looks out the window. "No."

"Charlotte ..." I make a fist with my hand. "It's in your best interest to do what I want. Or do you want to stop eating altogether?"

I know she's hungry. I've seen her clench her belly and noticed how she keeps ignoring her growling stomach. She ignores the need for nutrition because it's her only way to control what's happening to her, and she uses it as a weapon against me. But I won't allow it anymore.

"Either you do this, or you can die from hunger. Your choice," I growl.

I mean it. I'm done playing her games.

She loudly sucks in a breath through her nose and licks her lips as if she needs to get rid of a foul taste. "I apologize," she says under her breath. Her voice soft as a feather and almost inaudible, but I heard it. "And I promise not to do it again."

A wicked grin spreads on my lips. "Do you still want clothes? Or should I drag you down the aisle in your birthday suit?"

She looks at me at in disgust. "What?"

"You heard me." I cross my arms over my chest. "You want to wear clothes to our wedding? Ask me, and maybe I'll let you …"

She scowls once again and refuses to look me in the eyes as her lips part. "Fine. Please, can I wear some clothes to my goddamn wedding?"

"No," I say, narrowing my eyes. "Beg me like you mean it."

She takes another deep breath as though she feels humiliated. Good. I want her to feel that. I want it to sink into her bones so she'll never forget. So she'll think twice before she throws a tantrum.

"Can I please wear clothes?" she asks, this time without the begrudging tone.

Fuck. I love hearing her grovel. I could get used to this … I definitely could.

I approach her again and place a hand on her head, petting her hair. "Good girl. Now go make up to Jill, and then we can all get on with our day."

When I press a gentle kiss onto her cheeks, she completely freezes. By the time I move away, she still sits rigidly on the bed and doesn't even look me in the eyes as I open the door and close it while making the last eye contact.

I know my lips and touch can be overwhelming. She'll get used to it soon.

***

Charlotte

A few days later

"Stay still. It'll only hurt for a few seconds," the man says as he sits down on a stool beside me.

My hands clench together in an effort to stop the tears from forming in my eyes. Easton's standing right in front of me, and he watches while the man places the wet cotton against my ear and then a sharp tool. I can't look away, but I don't want to look at Easton either. Instead, I close my eyes as the sharp tool punctures my earlobe and a piercing pain emanates throughout my ear.

"All done. Easy, right?" the man muses as if it's nothing. "Now the other side."

I don't even know his name or why he's doing this to me. Doesn't he know I'm not here because I want to be? That he's doing something against the law?

Piercing my ears without asking me if it's okay … exactly what I'd expect from a man like Easton. Vicious to the bone. He glares at me like a man obsessed. As though he's marking his property. I'm like a cow getting branded, and it makes me want to explode.

But Easton's vigilant eye stops me. He's only here to keep watch, in case I try to say something to this man piercing my ears.

Still, I hate sitting here without saying a word while my second earlobe is pierced. It burns like fire, and my whole body shakes with rage when it's over. With a tepid smile on his face, the man picks up a small mirror and holds it up so I can see. Two sparkling diamonds flaunt my ears. I've never had earrings before, and if you ignore the stinging, they don't look so bad. Except for the fact that no one asked me what I wanted, of course.

"Perfect," Easton says to the man.

"Clean it every day with this solution," the man says, handing a tiny bottle to Easton. "And make sure she doesn't touch them too much."

Easton nods at the man, and says, "My assistant will take care of the payment. She's downstairs."

"All right," he says. "Thank you for your business, and I hope you enjoy your new earrings, ma'am." He smiles once more before packing up his things and leaving the room.

While I remain seated on the chair, Easton goes to close the door. I fiddle with the earrings while my eyes are fixed on the small hand mirror. I'm only a prize, a part of Easton's collection adorned with diamonds and gowns. A pretty little doll he can dress and play with.

A hand rests on my shoulder. Easton appears in the mirror, wearing a lopsided grin. Like the devil himself, he brings his lips to my ears, and whispers, "Beautiful."

The sound brings chills to my skin, causing all the hairs on my neck to rise.

Suddenly, he places a soft kiss on my neck. I freeze, my muscles tightening. His lips drag up all the way toward my earlobe, where his tongue dips out to lick up a tiny speck of my blood.

Fuck.

Why does my body send out such mixed signals? I hate it.

"They look riveting on you," he murmurs into my ear. "Don't you think?"

I can't even focus on what he's saying. My mind is still reeling from that kiss. But it's wrong, so wrong … I can't give in to his demands, no matter how sinful those lips felt on my skin.

I swallow away the lump in my throat. "It's fine."

"You don't like them?" he asks, swiping aside my hair as he watches me through the mirror. "There are plenty of other earrings to choose from once these have healed. I can arrange for Jill to bring them over so you can choose. Would you have preferred pearls?"

"No. This is fine," I lie. I don't want to spend any more time on this. I don't want to be happy, and I don't want to make him happy either.

"Good." He squeezes my shoulder. "I want you to be

happy."

That's not true, and he knows that, but he doesn't care. He wants to think I'm happy so he can live with what he's doing to me, but I won't ever forgive him.

He leans forward and kisses me on the cheeks again, adding, "Soon, you'll be mine alone just as you were meant to be from the start. And then you'll beg me to take your cherry, princess."

My eyes widen as he leaves me and closes the door behind him, his last words repeating in my head.

Cherry … my virginity.

Something I'd completely forgotten about because I never dated guys. I was too busy working to make a living, and I was afraid my father would find out and hurt them, so I never even tried.

And now my first time ever having sex will be with my captor.

Fuck.

TWELVE

Charlotte

I can barely breathe.

Not just because my corset is on so tight so they can hoist me into the wedding dress he selected for me … but also because I'm terrified. Terrified of the sparkling studs on my chest, the high-heeled peep toe pumps on my feet, the tiny silver tiara on my head, and the veil that hangs low over my curled hair.

These past few days have felt like a blur. I'm shaking as I stare at myself in the mirror, at that woman I've been forced to become. A woman who's about to marry her biggest enemy. A man who took her as a prize.

Princess … he uses the name as an insult, but that same princess stares right back at me through this mirror. A princess who doesn't belong in these shoes or these clothes, yet she has no choice in the matter. She's getting married to the devil as payment for her father's debt.

It's hard to sigh when you don't have any room to breathe, and someone is pulling and tugging on your bodice, trying to fit you into the outfit they made from scratch by hand. I don't blame Jill for trying; she had to make it work within a few days. That's all the time he gave her … all the time he gave *me*.

I should be protesting, screaming my lungs out, and punching my way through the door to get out. Instead, I'm just standing here staring at myself while I get dressed up as a dolly once again. If I fought Jill, he'd probably punish her instead of me and then force me to watch to make me feel guilty.

And I don't wanna go through that again. I already apologized once the last time I acted out. I won't let him humiliate me a second time. Right now, I'm letting it all happen, just like the tears that are a blink away from tumbling over my cheeks.

"Look at you!" she says when she's finished. She's radiating. "God, you look so beautiful."

I give her a fake smile. "Thanks."

"Well, go on, spin for me," she says, clapping her hands like a little girl.

I tap my feet and do what she asks, never taking my eyes off the woman in the mirror who I don't even recognize anymore.

"Perfect! What do you think?" she asks. "Do you think it's too much?"

"No … I like it," I lie. I can't bear to hurt her feelings again the way I did last time. I may be a princess, but this princess has morals too. Hurting someone twice in a row isn't something I stand for, even if she knows what she's doing isn't right.

She smiles, tears appearing in her eyes before she grabs my bouquet for me, and says, "Here. Hold it." Before I can reply, she shoves it into my hands and snaps a shot with a Polaroid, waving the photo in front of me. "Look at you. So pretty," she murmurs as we both stare at the shot. But all I see is a pretty girl trying to hide her misery.

"Oh, look at the time!" she exclaims, glancing at the clock before snatching the photo from my hand and tucking it into her pocket. "We need to get you ready to go."

By go, she means walk down the aisle.

Have a ring put on my finger.

Get married.

The thought makes my heart drop, and my stomach feels as if it's doing a corkscrew.

"C'mon, everyone's probably already waiting for you," Jill says, hurrying me out of the room.

Before I know it, I'm in the giant hall, right in front of the door that'll open in a few seconds and lead straight to the altar. I'm ready to hurl, but I have to keep it together for the sake of my pride. For my father, who's sitting in one of the front row seats along with my brother, eagerly awaiting my arrival and marriage to this cruel man. He didn't even want to walk me down the aisle. But it doesn't matter.

No one cares about what I think or what I want, and I have no choice. Either I do this or my father perishes, and probably a load of other people too if Easton doesn't get his way.

So I take a deep breath, lift my head high, and strut toward the door in my expensive long-sleeved, laced up mermaid gown, determined not to cry.

***

EASTON

When she appears from behind the closed doors, she takes my breath away. I didn't see her beforehand because I'm old-fashioned like that, but she looks drop-dead gorgeous. Jill did her best for Charlotte with this spectacular mermaid wedding dress.

She walks down the aisle with flair and her head held high, her footsteps soft and poignant like a fierce lioness. She doesn't look anyone in the eye … except for me. Her face doesn't adorn a smile, but the way she looks at me …

burns as hot as the sun.

I can't stop the grin from appearing on my face with the knowledge this woman is about to become my wife. That, in mere minutes, I will put a ring on her finger and kiss her on the lips for the first time ever.

My Charlotte … No longer a Davis, she will finally be a Van Buren.

Until death do us fucking part.

***

Charlotte

My head spins from all the eyes honed in on me. I'm like a goddamn bomb about to go off. But my legs push me forward and bring me toward the altar to the man who will take my life and never give it back.

I'll lose myself forever here … and I'm letting it happen without even fighting back. I should run, hide, do something.

Instead, I stand before my captor and let him take my hand.

Everything that follows is a blur.

A person talks about our history, our past, our future,

but none of it registers. People rejoice, and everyone seems happy, so I don't understand why I feel so dead inside. Why I go deeper into that pit of despair the longer this goes on.

My brother sits right in front of me, but he never looks me directly in the eyes. My father brings forward the rings. The sight of his face makes me want to burst into tears, but I keep it together for my own dignity. For my honor, my self-worth. My father sold my soul so he wouldn't have to die … can I truly be mad at him? Or would I have done the same?

The proud look in his eyes and the kiss he plants on my forehead make me tremble, make me question everything I thought I knew about myself, and it grounds me. Him being here forces me to focus on the reason I'm doing this. Not just because I have no choice in the matter, but because this is the better option.

But no matter how hard Easton tries to make me look at him like I did while I walked down the aisle, I refuse. Not as he holds my hand and professes his love, and not as he takes the rings from my father.

I want to run. Scream. Leave this place and never come back.

Maybe I should.

There's still time.

Would they be able to catch me? To hunt me down before I'm gone?

Guards are scattered around us. One. Two. No, five. Never mind, more than that, maybe a dozen … or two. Could I escape them all, and would they let me go if I told them the truth?

I, Charlotte Davis, am about to marry a man against my will.

Who would fight for me? Who would defend my honor?

A few more seconds pass, and Easton holds out my shaky ring finger to slide on the ring.

People clap and smile at us, and before I know it, Easton's placed his lips on mine.

For a moment, I forget everything that's happening; everyone and everything around me disappears into the distance. All that's left are me and him and his mouth on mine, drowning away all my regrets, all my sorrows, all my worries.

And then he takes his lips off mine, and the buzzing feeling wakes me up from the haze, reminding me what just happened.

Tears roll down my cheeks. "Don't cry, princess. You're mine now," Easton whispers, and he brushes them away with his thumb. He holds up my hand in the heat of the moment. "Charlotte Van Buren, my wife," Easton says proudly, and the room claps once again.

Wife.

Charlotte Van Buren.

Those two sentences make me realize I'm too late.

It's too late to run. Too late to hide. Too late to pretend this never happened.

Because it already did, just like that.

I'm married now, and my life as I knew it … is over.

THIRTEEN

EASTON

The reception ended fast, just the way I like it, with a few gifts sprinkled here and there courtesy of our guests. I don't want to waste time on celebrations when I can finally be alone with her ... my princess ... my wife.

With Charlotte Van Buren finally mine to ravish, I can't wait to get my hands all over her. A honeymoon isn't necessary. My mansion will do just fine as I have plenty of ways to spoil her there.

We're in the limo on our way back home, and my hand can't stop drifting toward her. I caress her soft arms and slide my hand on top of the fabric of her dress, petting her leg and squeezing it softly.

However, she moves away, clenching her legs as she gazes out the window as if pretending I'm not there. But we both know she's only avoiding the inevitable. Now that she's my wife, I have every right to claim her, and she knows this.

She's holding off because she's scared, but that's okay. I'll teach her everything she needs to know ... I may be only a few years older than her, but I have enough experience to know how to make her go crazy.

First, I need to open her up to the idea. Plant a seed of hesitance so she'll start to doubt her own resilience against my seduction ... and then I'll pounce.

My finger trails along her soft cheeks and earlobe as I admire the diamonds in her ear. They look gorgeous on her, just as everything else she wears. "You looked so pretty out there today. I couldn't stop looking at you."

"Is a compliment supposed to make me feel better about this? Because it doesn't," she retorts, trying to shift her neck farther away from me, but it only allows me to move closer and caress her neck fully.

"You should be thankful your father's still alive," I tell her.

"Oh, I am, but that's not thanks to you," she says, licking her lips.

If she thinks she has a say in things, I've got news for her because I'm the one in control. I cup her chin and force her to look at me. "If he's alive, it's only *because* I let him live. That's my mercy. Do not mistake it for your power."

She jerks free as we arrive at my home. I get out she

immediately bursts out after I open her door. I follow her inside, and we stomp up the stairs, where I attempt to grasp her hand. She pulls away and storms to her room.

She may think this is all fine and dandy, but this conversation and my appetite for her are far from over.

***

Charlotte

"Leave me alone," I say, trying to get away from him, but no matter where I go, he follows me. I can't escape, no matter how badly I want to. *Fuck*.

"You're my wife now, Charlotte. It's time you started behaving," he replies, following me into my room. With him, nothing is private, nothing is sacred, and that scares me … but at the same time, my heart is in my throat at the thought of being in the same room with him.

I cannot give in. My pride is worth more than a ring on my finger.

I spin on my heels, my arms folded as I glare at him. "Yes, I *am* your wife." Saying that out loud sounds dirty. "You got what you wanted. What else is there to give? I have nothing left."

"Yes, you do …" he murmurs, stepping closer into my comfort zone. I grow rigid immediately, overcome by the sheer force of dominance he exudes. "And there is so much more that I want from you." He tips my chin up, and whispers, "Now kiss me like a proper wife."

As he tilts his head ever so slightly, waiting for me to act, I swallow hard and think about it. If I don't do what he wants, we both know what'll happen. But how far am I willing to let this go? How far can I take it before I lose myself?

Judging from the smile on his face, he knows he has me where he wants me. Fuck.

"Anxious, little princess?" he murmurs with those enticing, deadly lips of his.

"Not at all," I lie, and I close my eyes and give him the smallest of pecks on the cheek. "There you go."

"Tsk … on the lips, princess," he mutters, biting his bottom lip. "Here, let me show you how it's done."

Before I know it, he's leaned in and pressed his lips on mine. He kisses possessively as if he wants to own my whole body, and I can't imagine what he would do with those lips somewhere else. Fuck. I shouldn't even be thinking about this.

He took me by surprise, and I'm completely irked at how I let him kiss me, so my instinct takes over, and I bite his bottom lip.

"Ouch." He inches back, touching his lip with his index finger. A droplet of blood rolls down, and his tongue darts out to lick it up. A soft moan escapes his mouth, and it sets my body on fire. I hate the way my body responds to his kiss and the sounds he makes. It's wrong, and it can't happen again.

Except he immediately grabs my hair, pulls back my head, and plants his lips on mine. This time, he's much fiercer, much more controlling. It's as though he's suddenly shifted personalities, and the devil has replaced his sweeter side. This is the man who I fear, the man who I loathe ... the man who can consume me. For every second his lips are on mine, I lose my sense of reality and time. All I can think of is how overwhelming it feels, and my mind turns to mush.

When his lips unlock from mine, I'm left reeling, dizzy, and completely out of tune. I'm so shaky, he has to hold me up, and his hand on my waist almost feels good. Almost.

"Is that how you like it?" he murmurs, still merely inches away from my face. His thumb slides across my cheekbone, my chin, and it dips into my mouth, pulling me closer, forcing me to lean into it. I don't dare bite because it wouldn't ward him off; it would only draw him closer. I've learned that much from our brief one on one tonight.

"You like your men assertive ... to take away your sense of control so you don't have to think about the guilt," he murmurs, running his thumb along my lips, smearing my saliva all over my chin. "You *want* to be someone's plaything so you can forget."

I make a face and suck on my bottom lip. I won't give

him the satisfaction of being right. "Fuck you."

A dirty smile appears on his face. "Typical ... but don't worry, princess. I'll definitely fuck you."

"As if," I hiss.

"Hmm ... You say that now, but you'll change your mind. Sooner or later, you'll give in to me. Just like you did when I kissed you," he muses.

I'd smack that smugness off his face if I could.

"But I'll wait because I wanna savor you," he murmurs, toying with my hair, "until you beg me to take your cherry."

"Never," I reply staunchly, but my voice is shaky.

"Very convincing, princess." He winks. Fuck him. "But we'll see soon enough how badly you yearn to submit."

Before I can spit in his face, he turns around and walks toward the door. "Take a bath. You look like you need one."

And he leaves the room and locks me inside alone with all my thoughts ... and a thrumming heart.

***

EASTON

I lean back in my comfy recliner. I wonder how warm she made the water and if she prefers bubbles or oil. If she likes the tub I had installed for her. What she looks like underneath all that fabric. Her soft, naked skin.

The number of layers on her huge dress surprise me. Maybe I should've told Jill to help her undress. I wonder if she'd allow Jill to help her or if she'd yell for her to leave. Charlotte doesn't seem like the kind of girl who enjoys being watched.

Too bad for her.

It looks as though she's managing quite well on her own. All that's left to take off is the tight corset around her waist. The pretty lace looks delicate, and a part of me wishes I was there myself to take it off. I have to take it slow, though, and give her time to adjust to her new status ... and to me.

I can watch her perfectly fine from here in my private study. My laptop has a direct connection to every camera in this house. Secured by a password, of course, since I wouldn't want a certain young lady snooping around.

No, I'll be the only one in this house who knows what's going on, and I'll be the only one who watches her undress.

Her clothes drop to the floor, uncovering a magnificent body. More beautiful than I could've imagined with its sinful curves and her deliciously round butt. I wonder how smooth her creases are, and what her moans would sound like if I let my hands slide up toward those already taut nipples.

Fuck. I'm getting hard from the thought.

She tiptoes around like a little fairy, touching the water with a single fingertip before inching closer and letting her foot slide in. Then she picks up a bottle and chucks in the contents. Oil it is. Maybe I'll introduce her to the bubbles next time ... when we get in together.

Like an elegant swan, she sits down in the tub and leans back, exposing her belly, her ample breasts, and her sexy legs along with that pussy that I yearn for so much.

My hand immediately moves toward the tent in my pants, rubbing the hardness underneath as I watch her bathe. She washes with a damp cloth, dabbing it all along her body with her eyes closed. It's as if she's enjoying herself, and I can't get enough of watching her do it. It turns me on like nothing else, and I bring my hand into my pants to masturbate to the sight.

I don't care that it's wrong or that she doesn't know I'm watching. I need to release this pent-up desire, or I'll take it from her instead, and we both know she doesn't want that ... yet.

Besides, my door is locked. No one can find me here, and I can enjoy her naked splendor all by myself, just the way it's supposed to be. My fucking wife is mine to savor, mine to cherish, and I will fucking take lots of pleasure in watching her.

My balls squeeze tightly as she parts her legs. I catch a glimpse of her tight pussy and imagine squirting my cum all over her. I wonder how she'd react. If she'd slap me ... or if it'd make her wet instead.

I know she likes it. She can pretend all she wants that she doesn't, but we both know it's a lie. I've seen her do it in her own apartment, back when she didn't know all the things I had planned for her. When I came to her at night and stole her laptop, I browsed through her history and found hours and hours of watched porn … including gangbangs and forced deep throating with lots of gagging and crying.

It's a secret fantasy of hers that she can't wait to live out. Once I remind her of it, and she realizes it's within her reach … and then I'll give her what she needs and own her. Body and soul.

But as I'm about to reach the edge, she suddenly looks up … straight into the camera.

FOURTEEN

EASTON

I stop jerking off as her eyes narrow, and she cocks her head almost as if she's only just noticing that she's being watched. But then she shakes her head, lifts up her middle finger, and continues bathing as though nothing ever happened.

Fuck.

My cock goes flaccid under my hand, and I pull out and zip up, groaning. Guess now's not the time to enjoy myself. Not when she knows I'm watching and doesn't even care.

Maybe this girl is tougher than I thought.

I click away and close my laptop, then put a cigar in my mouth and light it. I'll wait until the time is right. It won't take her long to finish her bath and climb in her bed … sleeping the night away …

Or not.

***

Charlotte

The brand of oil matches the one I have at home, constantly reminding me of the freedom I've lost. But the heat of the water makes it easy to ignore that.

At first, I hated the idea of taking a bath because it was his idea, but the moment I put my feet into the water, I was sold. Besides, it's not as if I could say no. If I didn't do it, he'd know with all those cameras in the house.

Of course, I knew he was watching. Since I discovered the camera in the kitchen, I did a little snooping in my own room and found several more. I'm guessing they're all over the house.

At first, I wanted to rip them all out and stomp on them, but I realized that would only anger him more, and I'm not eager to earn any punishments. So I went with the flow and pretended I didn't know.

Until now.

I wonder what his face looked like the moment I stripped and stepped into the bath. If he was all hot and bothered and couldn't stop fondling himself. If he wished he were here with me so he could wash me.

That sick son of a bitch got what he wanted, and I hope he liked the whole damn show. It's all he's gonna get out of me because there's no way I'll surrender. If I'm going to be a prisoner in this house, at least I can make him go insane. After all, it's no fun being the only one who's losing their shit.

Tears have no place on my face tonight. I refuse to let this day of ruined innocence and the stealing of my heart get to me. Instead, I smile against my pillow, knowing I've lived another day. And with that thought, I fall sound asleep for the first time in a long time.

***

In the middle of the night, I wake up feeling hazy, not knowing where I am. My head pounds, and I feel fuzzy. Must've drunk too much alcohol at the reception just to deal with being married, but I definitely regret that decision right now.

My skin prickles as I try to twist in my bed. But no matter how hard I try, I can't turn over. Something's holding me back. A hand on the small of my back ... and another one around my waist. And not just that, but it's moving and sliding down toward my pussy.

Fuck.

The moment my lips part, he moves his hand over my neck. "Shh … relax …"

Easton's right beside me, whispering in my ear, licking my earlobe while he rubs up against me. It's as if I'm dreaming right now, but he's fondling me. My half-asleep self can barely register the fact that he's lying here in my bed … touching me.

His hands slide along my shoulders and my collarbone, stroking my chest. He dips into my nightgown and slithers down toward my breast, avoiding it on purpose as if to make me greedy for more. And I am … I'm not even fighting him.

The onslaught of his touch on my senses is too much as he caresses my entire body while kissing me, and my resolve breaks inch by inch.

"What are you doing?" I mutter, barely able to get the words out.

"Kissing you … loving you," he murmurs, planting kisses all over my neck.

I'm powerless against his assault. It's as if my body refuses to move, despite my brain telling me to do something. To tell him to fuck off and get out.

But I don't.

Even though I can talk and squeeze the blanket as he kisses my shoulder while he caresses me… I'm even getting wet.

Why do I let this happen? I hate him.

But at the same time, I'm not even sure I want him to

stop. My body resonates with the things he's doing, the way he touches me, and I'm completely taken over in the moment by his domination.

I belong to him. I gave away my life so my father could live his.

My body is Easton's to do with as he pleases. And now he wants it.

Is this because of what I did in the tub? I drew him toward me and made him come to my room. Why did I have to act out like that? Stupid, stupid Charlotte!

"Yes, that's it. Give in to me, Charlotte," he murmurs into my ear.

He grips my wrists and pins them together above my head while he's toying with me. I'm confused, completely dumbstruck by all the emotions and sensations coursing through my veins.

I've never felt anything like this before, not with any other boy I've been with, and it terrifies me to the point of being unable to resist.

"You want this, Charlotte. Admit it," he growls, rolling on top of me. "Shouldn't have taunted me in that tub. But you knew what you were doing. Well, now you have me."

The wicked smile on his face makes my heart pound faster. But before I can form a coherent reply, he's already smashed his lips onto mine. His kisses are all-consuming and numbing, as though I'm diving into a deep sea and don't need to come up to breathe. It's thrilling, unlike anything I've ever experienced before. I'm delirious from the way he claims my mouth as if it always belonged to him.

When he unlocks his lips from mine, I suck in the air, my lips tingly and greedy for more. But I refuse to ask. I refuse to give in to this jackass of a man with the smoothest tongue skills I've ever experienced.

And just like that, he slips off me, crawls off the bed, and disappears from my room as if he was never here in the first place. I'm utterly confused, staring into the hollow space he left as if that'll make him come back. Even though I tell myself I don't want him to. My mind is reeling from the nerve he had to touch me like that, yet my body is zinging in the remaining pleasure that's ebbing away.

Just like my resolve.

FIFTEEN

Charlotte

When morning comes, I still feel tired. I counted every hour on the clock. I've never been this anxious, but I couldn't stop staring at the ceiling as my body continued to hum to his tune.

Fuck him.

I'm so angry because of what Easton did … for toying with me and then leaving me high and dry. Why? What was the point? Did he suddenly regret what he was doing, or did he want to make me feel all confused?

I growl to myself, annoyed that I don't know the answer and can't look into his head to find it either. As the smell of freshly baked bread reaches my nostrils from all the way down in the kitchen, I jump out of bed and put on a bathrobe.

Without thinking it over, I storm out my room. My head is clear, and I no longer feel groggy, so I'm ready for a fight. Maybe it's foolish to confront him, but what's he going to do about it? He's already got me, and he thinks he can do whatever he wants, so it can't get any worse.

I walk down the stairs in my bathrobe and tie the knot around my waist well enough so he can't wriggle his fingers inside while we talk. A part of me tells me to turn around and go back—to stop this before it goes too far—but I can't let this go.

When I walk into the dining area, Easton's already sitting at the head of the table, reading a newspaper while drinking a cup of coffee as if everything is fine and dandy. He doesn't even acknowledge me as I step closer and place my hand on the table, sliding it all along the edge as I walk to the other end and sit down there, staring at him. He doesn't budge.

I'm momentarily distracted by the fact that my favorite magazine, *QT*, is lying right in front of me. I almost grab it, but then stop myself before I do. I can't give in to temptations, however small. Besides, it's awkward that he has the same magazine I always have at my home. Does he know what I like? Or is he going to randomly place a new magazine in front of me every day until I give in, so he learns what I like?

When the waiter comes in with our food, Easton looks up from his paper, and says, "Great. Smells amazing." He clears his throat and closes the newspaper, folding it neatly before adding, "Could you pour another cup? It seems we have a guest."

"Of course," the waiter says, then leaves in a hurry.

I cock my head, still attempting to get his attention, but he's still slurping his coffee and checking his watch like no other. Of course, he's carefully but obviously avoiding me. Who wouldn't after what he did last night?

But one way or another ... we're going to talk.

***

EASTON

She's been here for only a couple of minutes, and already it feels as though everything's gone up in flames. As if her presence alone can suck the water out of the plants and her gaze can set the tablecloth on fire. She's looking at me, but I'm ignoring her. On purpose, of course.

I enjoy the heat coming at me from across the table. I don't need to look at her to know she's fuming. She's completely obsessed about last night. Who wouldn't be when this arrogant but handsome billionaire wants to get his hands all over you and touch you in places you didn't even know existed?

I don't think she was prepared for what she'd feel when I came close, and now she doesn't know how to handle it, so she wants to blame me. But I won't allow it.

No, I'll let her steam in her own pile a little longer. I can tell she's losing it by not speaking up. If she talks now, that means she'll admit I'm still present in her every waking thought, and of course, she doesn't want to do that.

I'm guessing she also doesn't want me to have the satisfaction of winning, but there's one thing she doesn't know about me ... I always win, and quite frankly, I already won the world's best prize the moment she became my wife.

"Good morning to you," I say, adding a smile to be kind.

She folds her arms and cocks her head at me in defiance. "Oh, now you talk?"

"I hadn't noticed you were here." That's a lie, but I love the rage that bursts out of her mouth whenever I annoy her. It excites me.

"Stop it," she hisses.

I knew she couldn't help it. She hates it when people ignore her. It's what everyone, including her own family, has been doing to her all her life. The only difference is that they never noticed they were doing it ... but I do. But she needs to learn to appreciate my attention before I'm willing to give it to her.

I start cutting up my toast, bacon, and eggs and take a bite, savoring the taste.

"So you're just going to keep ignoring me?" she says, licking her lips as I swallow.

"I'm not doing anything except eating. You should too if you don't want it to get cold," I reply.

"You were in my bed and kissed me."

Ah, there it is. The magical words that have been resting on her tongue since the moment she stepped into the dining room.

"Yes, so?" She's stating the obvious here.

She rubs her lips together. "So you're not even going to say anything about it?"

"What's there to say?" I raise a brow.

"Are you going to pretend nothing happened?"

"I never said that," I reply. "I'm not denying anything, and I won't even try."

"So you don't care that you lay down beside me and touched me?"

"That's what husbands and wives usually do, yes," I answer.

Her nostrils flare, but she doesn't say a word, so I continue eating my breakfast.

"Does it even matter to you what I think or feel?" she suddenly asks.

She still hasn't touched her food.

I put my fork down. "Of course, it does," I reply. "But

you need to understand that you're mine. And I take what I want, when I want it."

"Even women … of course …" She rolls her eyes.

"No." A lopsided grin forms on my lips. "Just you."

She narrows her eyes at me. "Lucky me."

"Yes. Lucky you. Now eat your breakfast before it gets cold."

She grabs her fork and knife and starts cutting into her bacon as if she's butchering a live animal, glaring at me with those charming eyes that are dead-set on imagining my head on her plate. But that's okay. I can take the heat.

"Lucky?" she murmurs under her breath. "Lucky?"

"You're lucky I didn't go any further," I reply.

Her nose twitches in that cute way it always does when she's mere seconds away from screaming. But she won't because she knows she can't manipulate me, and that only seems to infuriate her more. But I don't mind … I adore it when she gets all worked up over something she has no control over.

What she fails to understand is that it doesn't matter whether I touched or kissed her. What matters is that I take what I want when I want it, and she needs to accept that.

But I'm willing to be patient with her because I'm her first, and her body still needs to get used to the feel of a man owning it and the pleasure that comes with that. I'll keep tending to her, slowly pushing her like a flower yet to bloom.

Chewing a bite of my bacon, I take delight in the way

she looks at me. Memories of last night resurface. "Last night, you seemed to be enjoying it thoroughly…"

"What?" she stammers, almost choking on her bacon. "Nonsense."

"Right," I mumble. Does she think I'll believe that lie?

"You didn't ask me if I wanted you to," she says.

"I don't need to, and you did … otherwise, you would've pushed me away, but you didn't," I say with a smile. She looks irritable as if she's caught trying to lie her way out. "I could've gone further. I could've played with your pussy until you came," I say while stirring my coffee, and her eyes follow my every move. "Would you have liked that?"

Her shoulders rise as she sucks in a deep breath, her eyes widening the moment I used that word … pussy. She knows I claimed it and made it mine. And it's making her hot and bothered all over again from the looks of it.

She clears her throat and grabs her napkin, dabbing it against her lips as if to hide her obvious flush.

"I could've gone further, but I chose not to." I know I left her high and dry last night, and she hates me for it—hates the mixed signals from her body—which is exactly where I want her.

"Why?" she asks. "Why not get it over with?"

Of course, she'd ask that … because she secretly wants me to. Her body desperately wanted to be touched and for me to suddenly take it away was cruel.

But I needed her to be on that pivotal moment, the edge

of despair, where right and wrong blur, and she no longer knew which choice to make. The moment when she'd either scream for me to stop or for me to take her.

I pulled away right then because I want her to savor the feeling, to remember the moment... so she can make a clear and vivid choice and not one that's made in the moment.

Her submission must be a distinct decision in both her heart and mind.

And I'll wait as long as I have to until it sinks in with her.

"Because you're still a virgin, and I'm going to push all your buttons until you beg me to take your pussy... like a real princess would."

I don't know if it's the smug smile on my face or my words that make her throw her napkin on the table and scoot her chair back. I'm expecting a barrage of expletives, maybe even a knife thrown in for good measure.

But what I get is a girl standing up with her head held high as she walks out the door without saying a word.

SIXTEEN

Charlotte

I can't stay there. Not a minute longer.

I thought I could do this, but I can't.

Not when he taunts me like this every single day, pushing me and shoving me in whatever direction he wants just for the fun of it. He doesn't say those things because he means it. He doesn't truly *want* me; he just enjoys angering me, torturing me, and pushing me beyond my limits.

And I'm letting it happen. I'm letting this powerful, arrogant billionaire take over my thoughts just because his fingers were all over my body last night, and I didn't protest.

Not until it was too late—when he'd already gone—did I realize what happened. I should've stopped it, but I didn't. He knows I regret that, but now he's using it against me.

Fuck him.

Footsteps are audible behind me, and before I know it, someone's grabbed my arm and pulled me toward him. "Where are you going?" Easton snaps.

"I'm leaving," I hiss.

"Impossible," he says, chuckling as if it's funny.

"Fuck you!" I shout.

He raises a brow at me. "Is that all you can come up with?"

My lips part, but out of annoyance, I don't know what to say, and it only pisses me off further. "Gah, why do you have to be such an asshole?" I reply, shaking him off. "Do you enjoy torturing me? Pushing me to the brink of insanity? Is that what you want? A wife who's lost her mind?"

"No." He steps closer, his hands in his pockets. "I want a wife who obeys my every wish, and I want that to be you."

"Then you want something that doesn't exist," I reply, shaking my head.

"You underestimate yourself, princess." He keeps stalking me when I walk off.

"I'm not a princess," I say, and I gaze down at my bathrobe. "It doesn't matter what clothes you put on me, what bed you make me sleep in, or how many times you make me dress up. I'm not a doll, and I never will be. You should've invested your money somewhere else." I turn around again and walk around the rooms, jerking on every window I can find. There must be some way to get them to open, right? They have to air out this place.

"You're wasting your time," he says, leaning against the doorframe. "They're all locked. We have vents for air."

"I don't care." I won't stop searching until I find a way out. I'll never stop. Not even if he puts locks on all the doors and windows or chains me to my goddamn bed. I'll never fucking stop. Because if I don't, he'll have been right all along about my inability to resist him.

He's still following me around even as I go into his private study where he keeps all his books and memorabilia. "Why are you so obsessed with escaping?"

I spin on my heels, and yell, "Because I need to be free!"

Saying the word free causes tears to well up in my eyes. It's the one word that defines all the things I lost the moment my father decided to sell my body to the devil himself and I came to this place.

Because that freedom out there is the only thing that'll save me from falling for him. For that … monster. Easton Van Buren only cares about his own freedom and no one else's. But somehow, someway, the perpetuating gaze on his face doesn't strike me as that of a monster. In fact, it's the first time since we met that he genuinely looks dispirited, his face marred with worry. And the air is thick with unspoken words and desires.

"I can give you that on my terms," he says after a while, his voice soft unlike before.

But that's just it. I don't want it on his terms. His terms mean being bound to his wishes and his rules. Freedom means the idea that you can make a choice, and in this house, there are none for me.

"You are my captor. The one who keeps me as a prisoner. A toy to play with," I reply. "You can't ever give me freedom unless you let me go."

"You know I can't do that," he says, taking a deep breath. "So don't ask me that."

"Then you can't ever give me what I want. And I won't ever be happy here," I say.

The look on his face darkens as if he finally realizes that there's not just a price for me to pay. He too has to sacrifice something in order to get what he wants; my happiness.

"I *want* to make you happy," he says, balling up his fists.

"No, you want to own me. Big difference."

"I already do. It's not enough," he says, stepping closer while I move farther back toward the long red drapes in the back of the room. "I need more of you," he says.

"Too bad you can't fucking have it," I hiss. Shuffling around, I fiddle with all the drawers to try to find something I can use to my advantage. A weapon, a device, a key; anything to get me out of here.

"I'm not some slot machine you can insert coins in and get whatever you want out of it," I answer, still searching the room for anything of use, but he's locked all the important drawers. Fucker.

"You won't find what you're looking for, whatever it is,"

he says.

"Shut up," I hiss.

"No. Remember the way I kissed you, Charlotte? Remember how it made you feel?"

I don't want to. I don't want to think about it because that means admitting that I remember how it took my breath away. I slam a drawer filled with papers shut, and say, "Do you enjoy seeing me suffer?"

He mulls it over for a few seconds. "I won't deny that it excites me." He adjusts his tie a little. "But I also want to love you and wrap you in my arms. Yet you won't let me."

Him? He wants to love me? Ridiculous. All he's done so far is hurt me and use me for his own gain. How dare he put this on me and try to make himself the victim in the situation. "No one asked me what I want," I say. "You're not the victim here. I didn't ask to marry you."

I pick up a random stack of papers off the desk and look through them, trying to find something I can blackmail him with, but it's only random invitations to someone's party, a dinner, and a business proposition for one of his clubs. Discovering nothing out of the ordinary and nothing I can use pisses me off so much I chuck the whole stack off the desk, screaming out loud.

"Who would you have married then?" he asks, completely ignoring my outburst. "Was anyone ever good enough for you?"

"No one!" I scream. "I wanted to be *free*."

"Free ... all alone with no one to love you?"

"I don't care!" I'm beside myself, and I'm pretty sure my face is completely red by now, but I don't care about physical appearances anymore. Not in front of him. He's already seen it all in the bathtub, touched it all in the guest bed ... I have nothing left to hide from him. Nothing left that's completely mine and mine alone.

"I don't need anyone to love me ..."

"You don't mean that," he says with a sigh. I hate that he can shatter my beliefs with a single sentence. "Everybody needs love."

"Not this kind of love," I say as he comes even closer. In my blinded rage, I managed to wriggle myself into a corner of the room, and now I have nowhere left to go. Nowhere to escape to ... because I'd end up right in his arms.

"What kind of love?" he mumbles, lowering his head as he grabs my chin and makes me look at him. "The kind that makes you mushy, or the kind that makes your heart stop and your body tremble?" He softly plants his lips on mine as if to show me he can be gentle too. The first kiss he's given me that makes me doubt my own resolve.

When his mouth unlatches from mine, it's as though my whole world has shifted on its axis. His kisses shouldn't affect me this much, yet I can't stop my body from wishing he hadn't stopped.

His fingers slide down my chin and down my neck, all the way to my shoulders and arms, leaving goose bumps in their wake. "You're looking for the kind of love where a simple touch electrifies your body."

With his body, he pushes me against the wall, leaning in for another kiss. This time, his lips are on my neck, right below my ear. When his hand slips inside my bathrobe, touching my belly and cupping my breasts, I gasp for air. Sucking in a breath, I try not to be affected but fail miserably.

And he whispers into my ear, "The kind of love that steals your breath away."

His face hovers mere inches away from mine, and a stare-down of epic proportions transpires. "That kind of love? Because I'm more than willing to give you that kind of love." He bites his lip, and he's so close that I can feel his hot breath on my skin. The smell of freshly roasted coffee and crisp toast fills my nostrils, making me want to lean in and have a taste.

But I shouldn't ... not ever, not in my right mind.

"Love needs to be a choice. I didn't make this choice," I say underneath a heavy breath. I'm trying not to let him affect me, but it's so damn hard that I can't even push him away or stop him from trailing kissing across my collarbone. His hand wraps around my waist, pulling me closer, and the grunt that emanates from his body makes my pussy thump.

No, I shouldn't do this. It isn't right.

A sliver of reason returns to my brain, and I lean away from him, shoving him off me. "Don't."

"Don't what? Give you affection? Make your heart beat faster? Love my wife like I should?"

"Don't call me that," I hiss. I hate the word. Hate what it means and everything that comes with it.

"It's the truth, Charlotte. Whether you like it or not, you are now my wife. And it's time you understood what that means," he growls.

As he plants his hand on the wall above me, attempting to kiss me again, I kick him in the shin. He jumps around in pain, clutching his foot while I march off.

"Wait," he growls.

"No," I spit. "I didn't choose any of this. I didn't choose you. I didn't choose *us*. That was my father's doing." Tears well up in my eyes. "All of you men are the same. I'm just a puppet for their own pleasure."

He stumbles toward me, but I hold up my hand. Stopping in his tracks, he acts as if he's suddenly seen the light and knows when to call it quits.

So I add the finishing blow. "You're no better than my father."

The veins in his face protrude as he grinds his teeth and narrows his eyes, visibly upset. Nothing in this world is worse than the man I call my father, and he knows this. He knows it's the worst insult a man could ever hear. One I'm more than willing to throw at him to make him see the direness of the situation he put me in. How much of a bad man he really is.

And with my head held high, I strut out of the room, pulling the knot on my bathrobe tight once again.

***

EASTON

I should go after her and force her to stay and listen, but I don't. I'm nailed to the ground, frozen by her words. By the time I've come to my senses, she's long gone. Back to her room, I presume. All alone and probably crying too. Fuck.

Grabbing the nearest lamp I can find, I chuck it at the door, breaking it into pieces.

"Fuck!" I yell so loud that it feels as though the veins in my neck may pop.

I am not her father, and I will never be her fucking father. Can't she see? I'm trying to be nice, trying to be the man she wants, the only man she could ever need. Yet all she sees is this horrible demon that took her from her nest.

What more can I do to make her accept me as her husband? Showering her with gifts obviously won't work, and she refuses to acknowledge the growing effect my kisses and touch have on her body.

Still, she fights me at every turn, and it's infuriating. It's as if she knows nothing else but strife. As if she lives for it and it turns her on. Maybe it does ... or maybe it's her only means to gain back the control she lost.

Whatever the case, I must manage it like I always do. I

must subdue her and put an end to this struggle once and for all. But how?

I run my fingers through my hair as Jill comes into the room, and asks, "Are you okay, sir?"

"Yes, I'm fine," I say.

"Do you want me to clean this up?" She points at the broken lamp. I'd already forgotten about it.

"Sure, yes," I say, waving it off. "Just throw it away." I don't have time to think about random objects in my house breaking or not.

Jill starts picking up the pieces, careful not to make a sound. I stare at my bookshelves, wondering where I went wrong with Charlotte.

"Are you sure ... you don't want to talk?" Jill asks hesitantly, pausing between her words.

I tilt my head and sigh before I look at her. "I don't think I'm the one who needs to talk."

Her brows draw together. "I'm sorry, I don't—"

"Charlotte," I say, adding a tentative smile. "Go see if she's okay."

She nods and gets rid of the broken pieces as though she doesn't want me to see them. When she gets back, I say, "Jill, don't let her leave this house."

"I promise," she says, nodding with thin lips.

I know Jill doesn't agree with my decision or what I'm doing, but she knows it's not her place to voice her opinion. Jill knows she owes me that.

She gives me an unsettled smile before leaving me alone

in my own brooding misery. I grab a glass and pour in some gin, staring at the label on the back as I chug it down in one go. I'll probably finish this entire bottle before the day is over.

***

Charlotte

I search through my room, throwing everything out of the closet, the drawers, and the bathroom, leaving nothing unscathed. I need to find something—a key, a knife, a tool, anything—to break out of this goddamn prison. I don't care what it takes. I need to get away from this man before … before … I do something I'll forever regret.

He keeps pushing and pushing, coming closer and closer, and I can't handle it anymore. I can't take how badly my body wants to give in when my mind says no. It's wrong. He's my captor, someone who keeps me as a prize he took from his enemy. I'm nothing but a toy to him.

No matter what, I can't let this man consume me. He doesn't care about me or my heart even when he says he does. It's all lies to make me submit. Because that's what it's all about to him … my submission … my defeat.

He wants to see me on my knees as a testament to his win.

I won't let it happen.

By the time I've gone through all my stuff, leaving the room littered with clothes, brushes, makeup, and shoes, the only thing I've managed to find are a few bobby pins I cast aside the moment I came home from the wedding and took down my hair. But maybe they can be useful to pry open doors … or windows.

I slide across the room and immediately start working on the lock around the window, pushing the bobby pin into the hole. It keeps bending out of shape, but I won't give up. I'll keep at it the entire night if it means freedom is on the other end.

After prying for about ten minutes, something clicks, and the lock pops open. My eyes widen, and a smile brighter than the goddamn sun spreads on my face. "Yes!" I murmur to myself.

With two hands, I push open the window and stick my head out, checking to see if anyone's there. I close my eyes for a second, breathing in the fresh air that's enticing me to jump.

Maybe I should. Is there a ledge?

I check and find nothing but a few branches entwined in a wooden trellis placed up against the wall. It could function as a ladder, but I won't know until I try. What do I have to lose? My life's already been given away. Time to take a leap of faith.

I position one leg over the windowsill and place my foot on the wooden structure and push down firmly to see if it'll budge. When it remains solid enough, I add another leg while still holding the window frame. Even though it creaks like crazy, it doesn't break apart. Maybe I can climb down safely and then see how I can escape the property.

As my fingers release the window so I can concentrate on my footing, the door to my room opens, and someone bursts inside. "Hey, I just wanted to see if you were okay. Easton said you two had—"

It's Jill. And she's caught me right as I'm trying to escape.

SEVENTEEN

Charlotte

In a split second, our eyes meet, and hers fill with a kind of despair I've never seen before. Jill screams out loud. I almost let go of the wooden structure in shock but manage to recapture myself and clench my fingers around it. That's when I move. As fast as a rat trying to escape its cage, I shimmy down the trellis along the prickly vines that grow up against the walls of the mansion. The thorns scratch me everywhere, and my bathrobe rips after it catches on one of the thorns. But the fabric of my robe is the least of my worries with Jill's head hanging out the window.

"Charlotte! No! Come back here!" she screeches. "You'll fall!"

But I'm completely transfixed by the freedom within my reach. Consequences be damned, even the repercussions of what I'm doing are real. Escaping endangers both my father's and my life, but when I find him, I'm going to keep him safe. That's a promise I'll make to myself right here, right now as I'm fleeing for my life.

The moment my feet touch the ground, they take me away from the castle as if they have their own mind. In mere slippers, I manage to cross the garden and run through the grass and beautiful flowers along the thick trees and bushes scattered across the property until I come to an overwhelming fence that'll be impossible to climb. What now?

I spin around to try to find a way out. Another gate is not far from here, but my surroundings are suspiciously quiet and devoid of guards. They must be somewhere watching, right? Or are they taking a break now, and it's this the only time I could ever possibly escape?

With Jill probably rushing down to alert them, there's no time to think about it, so I run toward the gates with the speed of a gazelle. My bathrobe barely stays together, but that's the last thing I care about right now as I sprint toward the gates. Five. Four. Three. Two. One.

The moment I reach it, I grab it with both hands and start climbing. It takes me a few tries to get my feet on spots that allow me to push forward, but I refuse to give up. I'm not ready to give up hope or the freedom that lies beyond these gates. If only I could push just a little farther. I'm so close I can almost taste it.

Suddenly, hands wrap around my leg and drag me down the gate. I desperately hold the gate as a last sliver of hope.

"No!" I cry out in desperation while someone pulls me down, away from my only escape. Freedom slips right through my fingers as my feet touch the ground once again.

"Let me go!" I scream at the two, who seem to be guards employed by Easton. "I need to get out of here! I'm being held captive," I say to them. "Don't you see? Help me, please!"

Instead of acknowledging my pleas, one of them picks me up and throws me over his shoulder. Neither of them speaks, so I keep pounding on his back, trying to get his attention.

"Let me go, you asshole!" I yell, as the gate becomes farther and farther out of reach.

Tears well up in my eyes at the realization that my attempt failed. I'm not going to see the outside world even though, in my mind, I thought I would. I'd already prepared myself for facing the people outside—for talking to them, asking them for help, and begging them to take me somewhere safe. I'd seen it all in my head. Every moment from the time I climbed over the gate.

I was so close … I could taste my freedom.

And then it was all ripped away from me.

"Please …" I mutter, staring at the wall in front of me as

they're undoubtedly taking me back inside. Who would do this job they're doing? What price is high enough for them to ignore these wrongdoings against an innocent girl? They're being paid blood money, and none of them even care.

"Shame on you," I hiss, punching the man again. "I don't give a fuck who you are; you're aiding and abetting a criminal, you hear me?"

"If you don't shut up and stop hitting me, I'm going to make you," he growls back. "Understood?"

"Fuck you," I spit back, and I bite him in the shoulder.

He growls out loud and then smacks my ass harshly with his bare hand. I screech in agony from the searing pain.

"It's time someone taught you a goddamn lesson," he says, putting me down before we even reach the entrance. Instead, he's placed me against the wall outside the mansion near a side entrance covered by low hanging trees. I try to run off, but he holds me back with his thick arms while his buddy walks a few steps away and checks his surroundings.

"Easton's been far too lenient with you," the guy says, and he looks at his buddy who nods at him to give him the all clear.

I look up to find a camera overlooking the area, but it's not pointed at this spot. This man is using the single blind spot outside of the mansion to his advantage to come at me.

He steps closer, his hands on the wall, trapping me inside. There has to be something I can do, anything ... *The pager!* I could call Jill for help.

What was the number again? Fuck!

I reach for it in my robe's pocket, but the moment I fish it out, the man snatches it out of my hand. "No, no, little girl." He chucks it away like it's nothing.

The wind blows underneath my bathrobe, causing it to rise and expose my thighs, and his eyes immediately follow the draft. Biting his lip, he growls, "Maybe it's time a real man made you submit."

He grabs me by my hair and shoves me against the wall hard, and I groan in pain. My eyes widen when his hand immediately moves to my throat and squeezes tight, trapping the air in my lungs. His other hand rips open my bathrobe, exposing my naked body.

"Don't make a fucking sound …" he grunts into my ear. When his tongue dips out to lick me, I'm ready to hurl. My stomach clenches as he unbuckles himself and zips down. I feel completely powerless and shocked, and I can't fucking move or fight him off as he spins me around, shoving me up against the wall.

Tears spring into my eyes as this bastard pushes up against me, whispering, "Spread those pretty legs for me, little girl …"

Suddenly, a loud bang makes me close my eyes, and I cover my face with my hands. There's complete silence, followed by another bang and then hysterical screaming. My eyelids crack open again, and the bloody scene in front of me makes me do a double take.

Easton's right in front of me with his arm stretched out,

hand curling around my arm, protecting me behind him. In the other, he holds a gun. The man who was about to force himself onto me lies on the ground mere inches away from my feet with a bullet wound right through his head. The other guard lies on the grass a few feet away, squirming in pain. Blood oozes from his abdomen.

"Fuck!" the man yells, grasping at his wound.

"You're lucky I only gutted you instead of putting a bullet through your head like your accomplice here," Easton spits on the dead body lying below us.

"I didn't do anything!" the guy yells.

"Anyone who tries to touch my property dies." His voice is gravelly, darker than I've ever heard him speak before, and it brings goose bumps to my skin. His grip on my arm is gentle, but I'm not scared of him the way I am of these two men.

Easton glances at my bathrobe over his shoulder, and says, "Cover yourself up."

I immediately grab the fabric and clench it around myself tightly, still shaking from the ordeal.

Easton approaches the man from behind and shoots him in the foot. I jolt from the violence. The man weeps and begs. "Please ... don't kill me."

"Kill you?" Easton laughs. "No, I want you to suffer. Just like she did when you decided you were going to help your buddy over there take what doesn't belong to you."

He covers his head with his arms as if that'll protect him. "She was trying to escape! I swear, we were only going to take her back to you …"

"No, you were looking for a spot to use her for your own despicable greed. How fucking dare you touch *my* princess?"

My princess. He claimed those words, licked them as if they belong to him just as I do, and it makes a cold shiver run up and down my spine.

"I'm sorry, I'm sorry," the man rambles. "Please, I wanna live."

I swallow away the lump in my throat as Easton cleans his gun with a steadfast hand. It's as if he didn't even break a sweat while shooting them.

The sky breaks open, and rain starts to pour down. More staff members exit the mansion, all appalled by the scene in front of them.

"Nick. Call the guys from the company," Easton says to one of his employees.

Nick nods and fishes his phone from his pocket before going back inside.

"Are you okay?" Jill suddenly whispers into my ear, and she places her hands on my shoulders. "I was so worried about you climbing out that window."

"I'm fine," I whisper back, trying not to alert Easton, who's still busy trying to take care of that one guy on the ground … and the dead body lying mere feet away from me.

"Why did you do it?" she asks while I start to shiver from the cold rain soaking my bathrobe. "You could've died."

"Because …" I shrug. What answer can ever satisfy her or Easton? Freedom is all I ever wanted but not like this. Not when I risk one of his own men attacking me… and for one of them to die right in front of me.

Jill picks up the pager from the ground and checks it thoroughly before tucking it back into my pocket.

After talking with a few staff members, Easton suddenly turns around to face me and looks me dead in the eyes. "Are you hurt?"

The bluntness of the question brings heat to my cheeks. I shake my head, still unnerved by his ability to change the subject this fast even though he just killed someone in cold blood. "A bit … rattled. That's all."

That's an understatement, but I don't want to put him further on edge by telling the truth.

He licks the droplets of rain off his lips, his intense eyes blazing with a fervor I've never seen before. He's soaking wet, but he doesn't even seem to care about the rain. "Did they try anything on you?"

"I …" His deep stare disorients me. I look around at all these people staring at me, and my throat jams completely. "I—" I stutter, my lips trembling while my mind contorts as it tries to twist these awful memories into something palatable.

"Jill," Easton interrupts. "Take her inside and make a bath. Get her clothed and fed."

"Yes, sir," Jill says, and with a warm hand, she grabs mine, and says, "C'mon."

The sweet smile on her face lures me back inside, back into that mansion I call my prison. But that same place calms me and allows me to breathe. Even though Easton's still outside while I'm being pulled inside. Even though he just killed a man and the mere thought brings shivers to my body. I don't know what made him such a violent man, but it saved me from a fate worse than death.

The melancholic look in his eyes is the last thing I see as the door behind me closes, maybe for good ... But I'm not fearful anymore.

EIGHTEEN

Charlotte

It's strange how safe and secure I feel in this place I shouldn't ever call home.

The guy who tried to claim me as his own is dead, and the other one is probably on his way to meet the same fate. The Company, whatever it is that Easton called them, will probably dispose of the bodies and deal with the aftermath while Easton continues his business as though nothing ever happened.

His staff must be used to this, but I'm not. No one's ever killed for me, yet Easton Van Buren didn't think twice to make that decision. He rescued me from an even bigger threat, shaking up everything I thought I knew about him. Twisting my feelings for him until even I don't recognize them anymore.

Am I truly thankful to this man who saved me from an even worse fate? Or is that the Stockholm Syndrome talking while one of his assistants undresses me?

"You're so cold," Jill says, peeling the bathrobe off my naked body and helping me into the tub. "This should warm you up nicely."

I sit down in the hot water and clench my legs together while she throws my bathrobe into the laundry bag. I hope she sets the thing on fire. "Please ... don't bring that bathrobe back. Ever," I say, and she looks at me as though I've lost my mind. "I don't want to wear it ever again."

"Oh ... of course," she says, adding a soft smile. "I can get you a new one. No problem."

"Thank you," I mumble, and I close my eyes and take a deep breath, trying to keep everything together. I'm still numb from what I just witnessed and experienced. Even as Jill leaves me alone for a second to take care of the bathrobe and grab new clothes for me, I can't seem to let my guard down. I can't break apart, not here in this house. Instead, I suck it up and push back the tears while staring wistfully at the wall in front of me.

Jill comes back and helps me wash. I don't need the help, but my body is not responding to any of my commands either. It's as though I'm nailed to the tub, to the heat circulating my body, trying to bring me back from the dead.

I almost escaped. Almost. And then I failed. Miserably.

The thought of how freedom literally slipped through my fingers breaks me physically, emotionally, and mentally. And on top of that, one of his guards tried to take advantage of me in the most despicable way. And then he died. *Bang.* One shot was all it took to end someone's life, and Easton did it as if it meant nothing to him. For me.

A strange mixture of sadness, disgust, and serenity flows through my veins. Sadness for the death of that man who disgustingly tried to take me … and the serenity that followed when Easton came to my rescue.

Did he know I was there, or did he hear my cries? Could he have seen me escape? Is he upset that I did?

My brain takes a second to reboot, and I chastise myself for allowing Jill to pull me back into the mansion. I should've pushed her away, should've fought tooth and nail for my freedom, yet I went inside like a placid little lamb ready for slaughter. All because of the way Easton talked to me. With that smooth, bossy voice of his, he can make me do whatever he wants.

I shake my head and look away. I don't want to see anyone right now, not even Jill. All I want is to be left alone, but she won't let me. Of course not, not after I decided I was going to jump out the window. They'll think twice before letting me out of their sight. Fuck. I should've thought of all this sooner and figured out a better plan.

"Do you hate it here that much?" Jill suddenly asks as she runs a sponge along my arms. When she reaches my hand, I pull back.

"I'm a prisoner," I reply. "No one ever wants to have their freedom taken away."

She bites her lip and continues to wash me despite my hesitance to open up to her. She's his assistant, after all. She likes him, obeys him ... can I even trust her? I have so many questions, and she's the only one I can ask.

"Do you think he'll punish me for trying to escape?"

She mulls it over for a few seconds while narrowing her eyes. "I don't think so." She pauses. "But he is mad at you, that I do know."

I sigh out loud.

"Don't worry. He's not as cruel as you may think."

"Right ..." I reply.

She keeps glorifying him as if he's so great, but she's seen what he's capable of too. Why does she think that's all okay? Doesn't she see the darkness in him?

"What about you? Why do you even help him do all of this? What do you gain?"

She sighs but smiles, nonetheless. "Mr. Van Buren helped me when I was in a tough position. I had nowhere to go, no one to ask for help, and he ... took me in, and gave me a job and a place to stay. I owe him my life." She clears her throat, and her cheeks flush a little. "If I have to be honest, I'm a little jealous of you."

I frown as she starts to clean my nails. "Why? Who on

earth would anyone ever want to be forced to marry a man?"

"I'm sorry, that was rude of me," she murmurs, tucking a strand of hair behind her ear. "I just mean that I'm very lucky he gave me a job. Mr. Van Buren can be nice if you let him." She's beaming as if someone lit her up and sent her off in a freaking air balloon. That kinda happy.

I narrow my eyes. Is she ... in love with him?

"Well, anyway, don't mind me," she says, brushing her thoughts off as she grabs a towel. "I'm only an assistant trying to do her best. And if you'd let me, I can be of great help to you."

"Right ..." I mutter, getting up.

"Just don't ever think about trying to escape again," she adds jokingly, but I don't find it funny at all.

"Don't you feel bad about any of this?" I ask as she drapes the towel around me.

"I always try to see the good side of things. And Mr. Van Buren has many. It just takes him a while to show them," she says, nodding. "But if you give him time, he'll show his true colors. Trust me, you'll warm up to him in no time, I promise."

I find that hard to believe. In fact, she sounds pretty much delusional to me. "Is he keeping you captive here too or something?" I ask as I get out of the tub and dry myself off.

She laughs out loud. "No, of course not, silly."

"But you're never allowed off the property, right?"

"I work for him 24/7. I can go off the property but not much."

"Then you're as much a prisoner as I am," I retort.

"Oh, no. Mr. Van Buren views me as his most trusted assistant. It's why I told him you escaped." She tries to swallow those last words, but it's too late. The awkward silent stare we share feels as if it lasts an eternity, like lightning prickling all around us.

"I-I ..." she mutters.

"Don't," I say, snatching the second towel from her hands so I can wrap it around my head. "Just don't."

"I'm sorry." She looks down at her feet as if she's unable to look me in the eyes. "Please, don't make me choose. It isn't fair."

As I walk past her, I whisper into her ear, "Life's not fair."

I sink down onto my bed and cocoon myself in the blanket, hiding beneath the fabric so I can be alone for a little while. I can hear her shuffle around the room, probably cleaning up after herself or trying to cover up my crimes ... I don't care. If she hadn't come into my room and screeched her lungs out, maybe I could've gotten to that gate before those assholes grabbed me. I'd be free by now.

Instead, I'm stuck here because she did what she thought she needed to do ... choose him.

It's always him.

Everywhere I go, everything I do ... it all revolves around him, and he knows it. He probably revels in it too. I wonder if he's going to punish me for what I did. If he'll punish her too for not stopping me in time.

A sudden click of the door alerts me to the fact she's left the room, so I lower my blanket to confirm. Finally, I'm alone. The first thing I do is check the windows. Of course, they're all locked again, and the bobby pin has disappeared. She must've found it and took it with her. Dammit.

I roll back onto the bed and gaze at the ceiling, wondering if there will ever be another chance or if that was my last ... and if I'll always feel this alone.

Jill is the only one I can talk to, but she's not a friend even though I sometimes wish she could be. But with one foul look and a judging voice, I chased her away. Maybe I was too harsh on her. After all, she was only trying to help me.

But she also destroyed my only chance at escaping too.

I grab the pillow and hug it tight as the tears begin to roll down my cheeks again. Fuck. I never used to cry this much, but I can't seem to stop. Not even as Jill comes back inside with a cup of steaming tea and places it on the nightstand beside my bed.

"Here, drink this. It'll warm you up," she says with a gentle smile. She seems genuinely worried about me, and the way she bites her lip when she looks my way tells me she's conflicted. Just as I am.

"Thank you," I mutter, smiling back.

I don't know why I smile.

I know I'm not the only one who doubts her own

decisions. And that we can all use forgiveness every once in a while.

***

EASTON

I spend the entire day pacing around my office, arranging to get rid of a dead body and one live one without too much notice. I didn't expect to have to shoot one of my employees and have the other one taken away, but I also didn't expect them to do something this heinous.

I should've done more thorough research into their backgrounds, should've done more to prevent what happened to Charlotte. They touched her; I just know it. Even though she says they didn't, I could see it in her eyes, the pain seeping right through them. It made my heart bleed to see her like that, made me wish I could take the pain away.

But I can't. Nothing I do will ever fix what I've broken or make this okay.

Enraged, I pick up a glass of rum and chuck it at the fire, roaring out loud.

"Sir, maybe you should rest a little," Jill says as she comes into my room to clean up the mess.

I close my eyes and massage my forehead with my

fingers. "I know. Thank you, Jill."

"You don't have to pretend to be kind to me," she says as she picks up the shards and puts them in the trash. "I know you're upset and rightfully so."

"She almost escaped," I say through gritted teeth. "And not only that but one of my own employees also tried to …" My throat jams up. I can't even fucking think the words, let alone speak them, without bile rising. I slam my fist on the table. "Fuck!" Jill touches my arm, but I push her away. "Don't touch me!"

She backs off and continues to clean my table and the glass off the floor. Her silence injects poison into my veins, filling me with that same guilt I thought I could temper when I first took Charlotte as my own.

The more I'm around Charlotte, the more I'm losing my hardened shell. It's as though the icy barrier I built around my heart melts away as time passes. But why? None of this should affect me the way it does, yet when I look Charlotte in the eyes, all I want to do is protect her forever. Kiss her, hug her, hold her tight, and never let her go.

But she's only a goddamn prize. A bodily exchange for money. Something I can use against my number one enemy to make him cry for mercy. These conflicting feelings make me do irrational things like throw glasses at the wall and yell at my assistant. Then again, she was the one who let Charlotte run in the first place.

"Could you have stopped her?" I ask Jill.

She gets up from the floor, and says, "No. She was

already out the window when I found her."

"How did she manage to open it?"

Jill bites her lip and fumbles in her pockets for a few seconds, but then she mutters, "I ... don't know."

I frown, gazing at her as she pulls her hands from her pockets again and continues to tidy up after me even though she's already picked up all the glass.

Something's up. "Are you sure?"

"She must've found something to pry it open with," Jill says, clearing her throat as she makes a neat stack of my papers and dusts down the chair.

"Right ..." I narrow my eyes. "Make sure you remove anything from her room that shouldn't be there especially things she can use to break out."

"Of course, sir." She nods, scrubbing everything in my study with a damp cloth, including my glass cabinets, as if she didn't just do this yesterday. But I have no time or patience for her conscience to suddenly butt in. I'm much more worried about Charlotte right now. Maybe I should go see her.

I take a deep breath. "Do you think I should go to her?"

With the cloth still in her hand, she turns around. "That depends ..."

"On what?"

She pauses and rubs her lips together. "Well, she was scared you might punish her."

I redo the buttons at the top of my shirt and readjust my tie. "Nonsense."

At first, when I found out she'd escaped, I wanted to. Desperately. I wanted to scold her, force her on her knees, and take her ass without mercy. I wanted her to beg for forgiveness.

Until I saw her face and the desperation that marred it ... and then I realized all I wanted was to take the pain away.

"Apparently, she believes you will," Jill says, and I can't help but notice the patronizing tone.

"Careful there, Jill," I retort. She may be my closest assistant, but she's still only that ... an assistant. She was hired to do whatever I wish. Nothing more, nothing less.

She blushes and immediately looks away. "Of course, sir. It's just that ... After what happened to her, she might've already learned her lesson, don't you think?"

She's so mouthy these days. I'm sure she means well, and I appreciate her honesty, but Charlotte is leaving a mark on her.

I look at the clock and realize it's already nine p.m. Nick told me Charlotte refused her dinner even though I would've liked her to dine downstairs with me. She's probably still shaken up from the ordeal. And now she's all alone in her room ...

"I'm going to see her," I say, walking off before Jill can refute my words.

As my hand hovers over her bedroom door handle, I close my eyes and take a deep breath. I can hear her sniffling from the other side. She's crying.

Without hesitation, I open the door. It's already dark

outside, and her room doesn't seem light. She's in her bed with the covers pulled up to her nose. But her eyes are closed.

I approach her and look. She's asleep ... crying. With no one here to console her.

Does she know she's crying?

Would she mind if I came to comfort her?

I crawl into bed with her and wrap my arm around her, burying my head in the nook of her neck. She's soft and smells of roses and fresh drops of rain, and it reminds me of my younger years, of a time when neither of us was stained by the pain of our past. A time when maybe, just maybe, we could've had more than a loveless marriage.

NINETEEN

Charlotte

In the middle of the night, I wake up to something wrapped around my waist. My eyes are sticky from crying, and I can barely open them. I'm groggy as hell. Still, I manage to turn my head ... and find Easton right next to me in my bed.

For a second, I'm frozen in place. My heart beats in my throat. He's sound asleep and snoring just a bit with his hand tucked neatly underneath my belly. I'm breathless and so damn tired still ... I just want to sleep, and if I speak, that means he'll wake up.

Do I really want to, knowing he's here hugging me instead of punishing me for trying to run?

His body feels warm and cozy against mine, and I can't help but cuddle closer into his embrace as counterintuitive as it seems. Right now, I could use the company in whatever way I can get it. Even if he is my enemy, my captor ... he's also my husband, and nothing will ever change that.

And with that thought in mind, I fall back asleep into a dreamless sleep once again.

***

The sun breaking through the curtains wakes me up. A yawn escapes my mouth as I crack open my eyes, but it's short-lived. There's no arm around me, and nobody lying beside me. Easton's gone as if he was never here in the first place.

But I couldn't have imagined it because I clearly remember him being here. Why did he leave? Did he not intend to stay after all and got angry with himself when he found out he'd fallen asleep right beside me? Or am I overthinking this?

Suddenly, I notice a note on my nightstand. I pick it up and read.

I've placed a new bathrobe and a pair of slippers in your closet, along with some new dresses and other clothes. Breakfast is ready for you downstairs. – Jill

A smile forms on my lips. I can't stay mad at her forever if she's going to keep showering me with gifts all the time. No wonder Easton enjoys having her around so much.

I get out of bed and put on the new clothes Jill bought for me. After checking myself out in the mirror, I still see that same girl being held captive as a prize, and my smile dissipates. No matter how many times I try to look in the mirror, I see the same gloomy expression every day. No fake smile will erase what's underneath.

I sigh and do my makeup before going downstairs. The scent of freshly baked cinnamon rolls and pancakes meets me halfway, and my mouth waters. Some of my favorite meals. Enticed, I go straight into the dining room. Easton's probably there waiting for me.

He's in his chair, but he's not reading the paper or drinking a cup of coffee; his eyes are honed in on me. Normally, he points at a chair or narrows his eyes at me while waiting for me to sit down. This time, he scoots his chair back and approaches me.

I stay frozen in place as he pecks me on the cheeks, and says, "Good morning, Charlotte."

"Morning," I say with an awkward voice.

I don't know how to respond. He's never been that kind to me. He's usually a grumpy bastard in the morning before he's had his first coffee. Is this some sort of trap? Is he only doing this so he can get something else out of me? I should stay wary of him. Even with all the pleasantries, I can't ever forget who he is.

He grabs my hand and leads me to a seat close to his. The table is already set, and by the time I sit down, the food arrives. There's no time to ask for anything; the moment I think of it, it's already been placed in front of me. But it doesn't sit right with me. It's almost as though he's bribing my mood.

"I wanted to start with an apology," Easton suddenly says.

Whoa. An apology? From him? That's a first.

"What happened to you yesterday never should've happened," he says.

My mind instantly flashes to the two men who grabbed me and tried to take me ... and then got shot because of it. My fist instinctively balls. I wish I could've kicked that fucker in the nuts before he died.

"I promise you, you'll be safe from now on. I will never hire people that incompetent again."

That's a bold statement. "How do you know it won't happen again?" I ask.

"Well ..." He clears his throat. "For starters, I'm going replace most of my staff with women. With the exception of a few men, such as Nick, who's been a tremendous help to me all these years. But he won't ever bother you, I can promise you that."

"Right ..." I mutter, narrowing my eyes. "What did you do to the other guy?"

"You don't need to worry about them." He smiles, but it

makes an icy chill run down my spine. From the way he's gazing at me, I'm pretty sure he killed the other one too … after torturing him for hours on end.

I swallow.

"Are you all right?" he asks.

He hasn't shown any interest in my well-being since I've been here, so why now? He's been nothing but a tormentor, yet every so often, he looks at me with completely different eyes. It's as though he can't make up his mind about what to do with me and what to think of me.

"I'm fine," I reply with a shrug. "For as far as that's possible, being a captive and all."

"Good," he says, ignoring the second half of my statement. "I want you to feel safe in this house."

I shouldn't ever feel safe around him … but strangely, I do. He shot that guy for me. Any threat to me is a threat to him, which makes him the safest person in the world to be around.

Yet the violence still makes me cringe.

"You shot him," I say.

"Yes, so?" he replies. "I did it to save you."

It's like he's trying to use the situation to flatter me. "You did it to save your property," I retort.

He cocks his head. "That hurts, but I guess I deserve it." He clears his throat. "At least you're safe and alive, and that's all that matters."

I frown. "When did you …?"

"What? Learn to shoot?" he fills in for me.

"It looked like you'd done it before," I say.

"I'd be lying if I said I haven't," he answers.

Well, that's a truth, for once. His eyes boring into mine say it all.

"I took some shooting lessons when I was still a youngster," he explains.

I narrow my eyes. That can't be all of it. You don't roll into killing someone that easily. "But you *have* killed someone before."

He taps his fingers together and sighs out loud. "Perhaps …"

"Tell me," I say.

He licks his top lip, and says, "It's not that easy."

"Yes, it is." I want to know what makes him tick.

He sighs again. "I … had to build my clubs from the ground up. That required some sacrifices."

"For other people, you mean," I say.

He bites his lip. I'm testing his limits, and we both know it. "If you want to put it that way, yes."

I grimace. "You killed people for financial gain?"

"I killed them because they deserved to die. Most of them were greedy bastards who only cared about money to invest in their golden toilets and sports cars. After they invested in my clubs, I told them I wanted to give forty percent of the profits to charity, and they all turned up their noses and laughed at me. They even declared me a fool."

Forty percent? Wow. He didn't tell me this. I'm impressed … and confused by my own reaction. He just admitted to killing people to advance his business, yet I'm not even mad.

"Most of them were coke addicted whore-bangers whose sole purpose in life was sucking out the soul of other people. I'm not sorry I killed them."

My eyes widen. "All of them? All of your investors?"

"No, just the ones who were too greedy," he says, leaning back into his chair. "But it was convenient. I could use their money without having to give them anything in return." A wicked grin spreads on his lips. "Except death …"

My stomach twists. "Why does it all sound so easy when you say it? You talk about death as if it's the most normal thing in the world."

"It is when you've seen it as many times as I have," he says, tilting his head down. "Close up, it looks like their glazed eyes are wide open as if their souls are stuck between here and the nether."

"You're sick," I say.

"I didn't choose to be this way, Charlotte," he says.

"Yes, you did. You could've let them live," I say.

"Bad things happen to bad people," he explains. "Or would you have wanted me to let that man who tried to use you live as well?" He raises a brow.

I swallow away the lump in my throat. I'd be lying if I said I didn't want that man dead. But I couldn't stomach the thought, let alone do it myself.

"Admit it," he says. "You're secretly grateful that I took

care of him. It puts your mind at ease doesn't it?"

Why does he read me with such ease?

"I do the dirty work other people don't want to do. Only hard work gets you where you want to be. If that means killing a few people, then so be it."

"But is it worth it?" I ask.

There's a pause before he answers. "Not one of those fuckers who died would ever give as much to charity as I did. I've taken their wealth and turned it into more wealth, then hand it over to those who deserve it. I'd say I'm doing the right thing, yeah."

He thinks he is ... but I can tell his soul is burning away like a candle losing its wax, and without fuel, that flame is going to die out.

I shake my head. "You're ruining yourself, Easton."

His nostrils twitch. "I'm done with this conversation."

Right ... Of course, he is. When it gets too hot under his feet, he avoids the questions once again. It's like he doesn't even want to face the person he's become.

"Did you sleep well?" he asks, grabbing a cinnamon roll and his coffee, totally glazing over the topic.

But there's no point trying to make him talk about who he is. If he refuses to speak, it won't get me anywhere, and the more I ask, the more annoyed he gets. So I have no choice but to go with the flow and let him lead.

I sigh out loud. "Yes ... you?" I ask, cocking my head as I tug the plate filled with pancakes closer to me and cut into them.

"Fabulous," he muses, a lopsided grin appearing on his face.

Of course, he did. He was snuggling me, which is what he wanted all along; to pretend we're one happily married couple. But I won't fall for it.

"You weren't in my bed this morning." My bluntness almost made him spit out his coffee. "Care to explain?"

"I don't have to explain anything to you," he replies, putting down his cup. "But I'll indulge you. I had important business to attend to. That was all."

"Right." I take a bite of my pancakes. Their deliciousness almost throws me off, but I force myself to swallow. "But that doesn't explain why you were in my bed in the first place."

He stuffs his mouth full of the cinnamon roll, and there's a pause while he chews and swallows. "You were crying in your sleep last night."

I raise a brow. "So you came to console me?" What a peculiar thing to do for a man like him. Maybe I misjudged him … or he has ulterior motives. Whatever the case, he must've felt *something* for him to lie next to me in the middle of the night and fall asleep.

Still, he refuses to even look at me as he's chomping away at his breakfast, sipping his coffee between bites like nothing's going on. He's hiding behind his food, and I don't like it one bit.

"Tell me," I say, slamming my fork down.

This catches his attention. "I didn't know you cared so

much about what I feel for you."

The way he hones in on me with those piercing eyes makes me weak. If I wasn't sitting right now, my legs would tremble underneath me. And I hate it. I hate that he makes me feel this way with just one look.

"I just want to know if there's something human inside you after all," I quip.

"Of course. But you don't want to see it," he retorts.

We stare each other down. "I don't believe it. And I don't believe for a second that *business* was the reason you left."

He takes an apple and cuts it into small pieces. "You wanna know what *I* believe? I believe you're upset I left you alone in your bed."

"Nonsense," I hiss, gobbling down my pancakes.

He smirks while chewing on a piece of apple. "Then why do you care so much?"

"Because you've never slept a night in my bed," I reply. "And I think it was an accident." He snorts, but I continue. "I don't think you ever intended to stay, and that you were shocked to find yourself lying in my bed when you woke up this morning. So you fled."

I grab a banana and lean back in my chair while peeling it. His eyes follow the banana as it goes into my mouth, and I take the opportunity to push it down as far as I can manage and then take a bite. I marvel at the slight twinge of pain on his face.

Yes, I went there, and I don't regret it one bit. For once,

he's on the defense. Good.

"So … what *business* did you have to attend to that was so urgent?" I say with a mocking voice while still pretending this banana is a dick. "Were you trying to trick someone else into getting a loan from you so you could force them to give you their loved ones too?"

He swallows, visibly agitated at the sight of me savagely eating this banana. Or maybe he's just angry I was easily able to pinpoint where the problem lies.

"As I said before, it's none of your business." He sighs out loud. "But if you must know, I do more than give money to bastards who don't deserve it. I also give money to people who truly need it. I love charities."

Oh, I remember him saying that once, but I don't, for one second, believe he cares.

"Why couldn't you just have loaned my father the money without demanding such an egregious favor in return?" I ask. "You could've made do with the money back plus interest."

He grabs a peach and leans back just like me. "Because you and your father needed to be taught a lesson." He brings the peach to his mouth and starts sucking on it. Hard.

And for some reason, it makes my pussy clench.

Fuck.

"I hate you," I say through gritted teeth.

"No, you don't. In fact, you're starting to like me," he says, licking the peach in an obscene way. Afterward, he takes a bite and swallows. "You only say that you hate me because you're stuck in this house." He takes another bite. "But maybe I'll let you off the property."

Now that's music to my ears. He's certainly got my attention there.

"If?" I add, wondering what the caveat is. Because let's face it, there *must* be one.

A devilish smirk appears on his face. "Lift your dress."

I frown. "What is this ... some kind of test?"

He cocks his head. "Perhaps."

Oh ... those games he plays are infuriating. But I'll play along, for now. If this means I'll get out of the house, then maybe lifting my dress isn't so bad. With my index finger and thumb, I raise the fabric until my knees are visible.

"Higher," he says, and I raise it even more. "Higher ..." he says again.

I don't stop until he tells me to, which he only does once I've exposed my panties. "Stop."

There's a certain gleam in his eyes.

"Got your fix?" I say.

"Not quite," he muses, licking his lips as he sits back in his chair. "Play with yourself."

TWENTY

Charlotte

My pupils dilate.

Wait. He can't mean ... now? Here?

"What? No," I say, snorting, but he doesn't seem the least bit amused.

"Scaredy-cat," he taunts.

"We're in the dining room," I hiss. "Anyone could come in at any moment."

"They won't unless I summon them," he answers.

Well, shit. That wasn't the only reason not to do this. I mean, I don't want to be lewd in front of anybody, especially not him. I knew he wasn't serious when he asked if I was okay. This was on his mind all along.

"Do you want to get out of this house or not?" he asks, blinking a couple of times as if he's daring me.

Fine. I'll take him on if that means I'll get to go outside of that damn fence. Maybe then I can escape his grasp.

My fingers drift up to my panties, and I rub myself through the fabric. His interest is immediately piqued, and he bites his bottom lip with glee. I almost feel empowered by his interest, but I mustn't ever forget who's in charge here ... who's forcing me to do this and why.

I push away any thoughts of sexual desire and focus on the task. I tell myself not to feel anything, not even as he starts to rub his own dick through his pants. He leans back, looking me straight in the eyes as if to tell me he knows I saw ... and he doesn't care.

He wants to show me who's boss, and he wants me to know the price of my freedom. If I want something, I'm going to have to buy my way there with dirty pleasure. It's wrong and completely evil, yet I can imagine it's the greatest turn-on to him.

In fact, I can see it with my own damn eyes ... the hard-on beneath his tented pants. I'd be lying if I said it didn't make me even wetter while I play with myself. I wouldn't ever admit that to him, of course.

"You look like you're enjoying yourself," I say, raising a brow to taunt him.

"Immensely," he retorts, grinning while rubbing himself

even harder. "But you know what would make it better?" he hums. "Put your hand down your panties."

I narrow my eyes at him. "Why would I do that?"

"Tick tock, Charlotte …" A filthy grin spreads on his lips.

My nostrils flare. "Will you keep adding new conditions to this deal?"

He laughs. "Oh princess, this isn't a deal. You need to earn your time."

God, sometimes I wish I could grab that glass on the table in front of me and smack him in the head with it, but that would only land me a spot in jail. He has assistants and employees around every corner waiting to come to his aid.

No, I need to do this the smart way, the sneaky way, just as he would. I need to get down to his level of scheming.

"Now earn my favor," he adds, spreading his legs so he can touch himself better.

I reluctantly dive into my panties and start massaging my clit. It feels wrong to do this here with him watching me, but I don't have a choice. It's either do this or stay inside forever, and that's the last thing I want.

He pops the button of his pants and zips down, shoving his hand inside his boxer shorts. When I get my first glimpse of his cock, I hold my breath momentarily. In fact, my jaw actually drops a little the moment he pulls it out fully erect. I don't think I've ever seen such a huge dick.

Not that I've seen many. The only experience I have is with porn … and the occasional boyfriends, but I never went further than kissing and touching with them because my father often chased them off. I've never gone as far as to watch someone jerk themselves off in front of me. And I have to admit it's doing something to me that I can't ignore.

"Are you getting wet for me, princess?" he murmurs.

I won't say it out loud—definitely not—even though my pussy clenches at the sight of his length. It's dripping with pre-cum, and he rubs it all over his shaft like lube while jerking off. The chance of getting caught by his staff probably excites him.

"Lower your panties," he muses.

Dammit, he keeps adding new rules. How long is this going to last, and how far is he going to push me? Should I comply or give up?

From the look in his eyes, I can tell he's testing my limits. As if he knows I'll give up eventually. I hate it, but I also want to prove him wrong.

I swallow away the lump in my throat and lower my panties all the way down and kick them off.

"Hmm …" The appreciative groan that emanates from his mouth as he looks at my pussy makes my cheeks heat. I hate that I have to do this to earn my freedom. And I hate that my own body betrays me.

***

EASTON

Like an expert, she toys with herself. It's almost as if she's done this before, but that can't be right. Her father assured me she was still a virgin, and from the way she looked at my dick, there's no way I can doubt his word.

Still, I can't believe she actually went along with it. That she's touching herself right in front of me and seeming to enjoy herself thoroughly from the looks of it. The apples of her cheeks are bright red, and she continues to avert her eyes from mine as if she feels caught in the act.

But I like this act. I like how she puts on a show for me, turning her fingers around and around. It gets me going like nothing else, and my cock is as hard as a rock right now. I jerk myself off until my veins begin to pulse, my balls tighten, and I'm about ready to burst.

Then I stop. My cock sways back and forth from arousal, and I catch her sneaking a glance before shutting her eyes again. I don't want to go too far too soon. I want to enjoy this a little bit longer, and I want her to watch.

"Open your eyes, princess," I murmur.

Her eyes flutter open, but she's still scared to look at me as if she's afraid I'll bite. Maybe I will … someday soon. But first, she needs to get used to the feel of being watched and owned.

Her legs clench together, and her body begins to shake.

She seems close to the edge. I revel in the sight of her touching herself for me. Does she dare go further? Would she come in front of me? It's been a wet dream of mine ever since I first laid my eyes on her back in the day. And now those dreams are coming true.

"Yes, bring yourself to the edge, Charlotte," I say.

She breathes soft and ragged breaths, her body quivering as she flicks her clit. Her bright, beautiful eyes focus on mine as she starts to unravel inch by fucking inch.

The moan that escapes her mouth titillates me more than I ever thought it could. Fuck. I wish I could hear that sound every day.

"Good girl," I say, and she sucks her bottom lip as though caught in a lie.

A lie she's telling herself ... that all of what we're doing has no effect on her. But we both know the truth.

Her skin glistens, and beads of sweat trickle down her neck and chest. Her peaked nipples show right through the fabric of her dress, and I wish I could suck them off. But right now, I want to use her in a different way.

I get up from my seat and stand in front of her with my hard-on, which she eyes as though it's a candied apple, and my tongue darts out in response to her desire. She looks up at me from underneath her eyelashes, and asks, "What are you doing?"

"I want you to suck me off," I say, my voice gravelly and strained from holding back all that arousal.

"I thought the deal was that I had to make myself ...

climax?" she mutters, shock settling on her face.

I smile and grab her chin, leaning in closer. "Deals change."

Her face darkens, and her brows draw together. "You bastard," she says through gritted teeth.

"Ah-ah, princess. You wanted to get out of the house, remember?" I release her chin and step closer until my cock is almost touching her lips. "This is the price."

"I thought you said you didn't want to take my cherry until I begged for it?" she retorts.

"Exactly ... your cherry ... but your mouth ain't that, princess," I muse with a smirk on my face, which angers her even further.

She knows I'm right. I'm savoring the thought of having her pussy for the time when she offers it to me freely. But until then, I'll make plenty of use of her other orifices.

She eyes me for a second, and I think I know what she's thinking. How far will I take this? How many times will I keep stretching the rules of the game? The answer is as many times as I want. That is what she needs to learn. I get my way whatever the cost.

Her nostrils flare again, and she sucks in a breath before parting her lips. Of course, she gives in. She wants nothing more desperately in this world than her freedom. I can use that to my advantage, but it's also a very pricy request, and she knows this. Every time she leaves my house, I risk losing her. So if she wants time out of this mansion, she has to earn every second of it.

I nudge her mouth with my dick, which prompts her to open farther and allow me entry. I slip my length over her tongue and enjoy the soft, wet feel. She narrows her mouth a little.

"Don't bite down," I warn.

She looks up at me with vigilant, almost cat-like eyes but doesn't say a word.

Instead, she begins to suck ... hard.

Fuck me, if I'd known she could do this, I would've fucked her mouth a lot sooner. As she wraps her tongue around my shaft, my head tilts back from the instant gratification. I groan in delight, all my muscles tightening. Fuck, I won't be able to keep this up much longer.

Guess I'll have to resort to plan B.

***

Charlotte

I can't believe I'm sucking his dick. That I'm willingly participating in this debauchery after almost escaping. This is so unlike me, yet here I am sitting in this chair, letting him take control of my mouth. I'm humiliated, and I can tell from the gleeful smile on his face that he loves it. He lives for moments like these when he can show me who's boss.

He thrusts slowly at first but then increases his pace. My own body has forsaken me because every time he slides inside, my pussy thumps with a need I've never felt before.

I'm so conflicted by the sensations that my brain shuts off and lets it all happen. I don't even fight him as he starts fucking my mouth as if it's just another hole. I wonder if he's done this to other women or if I'm his first too.

This isn't at all how I imagined my first time to be, yet here I am, being mouth-fucked by a billionaire mogul who wants to own me, body and soul. The longer this goes on, the more disgraced I am, but I can't stop it either, not even if I wanted to. His body pushes up against me. I could try moving my hands …

He suddenly grabs my wrists and presses them tightly together. He pulls his dick from my mouth, and says, "Ah-ah, princess … no touching." He unhooks his belt from his pants and ties it around my wrists, locking them in place. Fuck.

"Now keep that pretty mouth of yours open," he growls, immediately shoving in again before I can say a single word.

I'm being used like a fuck-doll, and nothing I do will stop him from wanting me in this exact position. Submissive. That's what this is about. The desire to dominate. I can see it in his eyes, the sheer frenzy at the sight of me beneath him while I'm sucking his dick. It's the idea that turns him on, not the act. And I was the one who handed it to him on a silver platter.

I should've thought about it before I said yes and let my desire to be free trump my rationality. Should've known this is what he'd make me do in return for a small escape into reality.

I gaze up into his pristine eyes that command to be watched and don't look away. I want him to see what he's doing, for my shame to reflect in his eyes and unravel him from the inside out.

But all it does is entice him even more.

He thrusts and thrusts, and I can barely stay in control. He goes so far down my throat that I can't breathe, and my gag reflex causes my eyes to prick with tears. Every time he pulls out, I suck in the air, only for him to go back inside again. My mind reels from the savagery I can't escape … and from the way my pussy thumps from arousal.

A loud groan escapes his mouth, and suddenly, a hot load fills my throat. I try to gasp but suffocate on his seed instead. I cough and heave as he pulls out and leans forward. His cum drips down onto the floor and all over my dress.

"You were supposed to swallow that …" he murmurs, lifting my chin so he can look at my face that he made filthy. A wretched smile appears in front of me. "Bad princess."

I can taste him on my tongue, feel him inside my throat.

He came inside me, and now my pussy can't stop clenching, and I fucking hate it.

Until Easton grabs another cinnamon roll and wipes it on my mouth, rubbing his cum all over it. Then he shoves it into my mouth, and says, "Now … eat up."

After staring him down for a few seconds, I take a quick, shallow bite and swallow it down. His cum doesn't taste revolting. In fact, it tastes more like some kind of strawberry dipping sauce. As if he meant to serve these cinnamon rolls like this all along.

"Now … clean yourself up," he says, zipping up his pants.

"And then I'm free?" I say.

He narrows his eyes at me while undoing the belt around my wrists. "Perhaps."

What? Did he just …?

My blood curdles.

"You *said* I could go outside," I say through gritted teeth.

He grabs a tissue and holds it in front of me. "Maybe. If you continue to behave."

I attempt to snatch the belt from his hands, but he takes a step back in response.

When he turns around, I yell, "No, this was the deal. You got what you wanted, and I'd be free to go outside!"

"Only good girls get rewards, princess." He walks out of the dining room without even looking back.

God, I fucking hate this man.

TWENTY-ONE

Charlotte

This mirror in front of me is my greatest enemy right now. I'm brushing my teeth over and over again, trying to rid myself of the memory of him. But no matter how many times I rinse under the faucet and scrape my gums with the bristles, I can still taste him in my mouth. That delicious strawberry taste that I know damn well isn't fucking strawberry.

I should've known that fucker wouldn't keep his promise. I thought he could be a gentleman, and he would honor his deals like he does when it comes to his business, but that was foolish of me. All he wants is to use me and break me, and he succeeded.

That son of a bitch blatantly took my mouth and owned it as though it always belonged to him. And I freaking let him like it was no big deal. Hell, I even participated by fondling myself right in front of him. The chance of being caught didn't stop me. No, I was blinded by my desire to be free and subsequently lost the game.

That won't happen to me again. No way am I letting him win again.

I should've bitten down his dick when I had the chance.

I keep brushing my teeth, trying to think of a solution to my situation.

Suddenly, someone knocks on my door and enters. "Ma'am, you're expected downstairs in a few. Please get ready." It's Nick, and he immediately closes the door again before I can respond.

Must be Easton wanting to see me again so he can bask in his victory. Fuck him. I'm not going. He can drag my ass out and rot in hell for all I care.

Or should I? Maybe I'd get a second chance at grabbing something sharp and stabbing him with it.

I don't know why I keep resorting to these violent thoughts, but they excite me. And it feels better to think about killing him instead of having to constantly remind me how he throat fucked me like some kind of porn girl. And that some deep, devilish part inside me might've liked it.

I spit out the toothpaste and chuck the brush into the

glass before exiting the bathroom. I come to a full screeching halt the moment I spot my favorite perfume on the makeup table. The same one I have at home.

"What the …?" I mutter as I approach the bottle.

This wasn't here before. Did Nick leave it for me to find? Was this Easton's idea? And how does he know so much about me? None of this makes any sense.

Seeing a note attached to the bottle, I take it off and read it.

Put this on plus a brightly colored dress. I want to show you off.

Easton

All thoughts about how awkward it is that he has this exact perfume sent to my chamber evaporate. Show me off? Are we going … out?

The mere thought of leaving this mansion and the property surrounding it makes my heart beat in my throat. I haven't been out of here since the wedding, and I've been dying to go somewhere, anywhere, as long as it isn't here.

I instantly forget everything I was doing, and I spritz some of my favorite perfume on my neck and the inside of my wrists. Then I open the closet and put on something new. A light pink maxi dress that ties around my neck. After I put it on, I check myself in the mirror. Perfect. Lightweight and not too flashy but enough to impress him … and easy to make a run for it in should the opportunity arise. Especially with these flats I'm putting on. If I find an opening, I'll take it. No questions, no regrets, not a single thought.

And with that in mind, I exit the room and go downstairs.

***

EASTON

When she walks downstairs, it's like an angel descending from heaven. With her pink hair and light pink dress floating behind her, she's like a dream come true to me. Everything about her is beautiful—from her pretty face to her petite body and killer legs.

Which is why I find it so hard to deny her the very things she loves. The things she craves, and the freedom she wishes for so badly.

I want to give it to her, but on my own terms and in my own time.

When we parted ways this morning, I knew she'd be mad at me for not giving her what she wanted at the moment. But I couldn't give her that because then it would give her the impression she's in control. I'm the one who decides when something happens and when I want to give something of value to her, and that moment is right now.

I hold out my arm and wait until she hooks hers through it before walking her out the door like a true gentleman. I know I can be an asshole, but I'm also her husband, and I will treat her like a princess when it's appropriate.

We walk to my car, and I help her get inside before closing the door. She glares at me as I go to the other side of the car and sit down beside her. By the time I've buckled up, my driver has already started the car and driven off.

She keeps glaring at me as if she's seen an alien or I've said something to her that shocked her to the bone.

I push the button to close off the front of the car to the back of the car so we can have some privacy. "What's wrong?" I ask.

"Nothing," she mutters, averting her eyes.

I frown. "You're looking at me …"

"I can't look at you now?" she scoffs.

"You can." I grab her chin and turn her head. "But not like that. Like you're hiding something or think I'm the worst man in the entire world."

"You are," she says, smirking at her own savviness.

I lick my lips at her comment. "Worse than your father, who sold you to the first bidder?"

Her nostrils flare, and she looks away, blinking heavily. I know I touched on a sore point there, but it's the truth, and she knows it. Her father couldn't care less about her, explaining why she's become such a stuck-up princess. Always trying to grab his attention and then right her wrongs when he wasn't pleased. Her whole life revolved around making her family happy.

Well, not anymore. She's mine now, and she needs to remember that.

"I'll be good to you if you let me," I murmur into her ear, and I press a kiss just below it. "If you'd just let me kiss you ... fuck you ... without fighting."

"No way," she hisses, but she still bites her lip as I place another kiss on her neck.

"You only say that because you think you should. Because you've been taught to act like a lady and defend against any immoral behavior. But you don't have to with me. I want you to be immoral." My hand slides up her knee between her legs to right where her soft spot lies. And she clenches her legs in response, her breath faltering. "Be sinful with me. It could be so fucking good." My thumb brushes over her pussy, across her sensitive areas, and it's becoming harder and harder for her to push back. She hasn't tried to fight me off. I can see in her eyes that a part of her wants to resist, but another part of her desperately wants to give in. That need to release herself from all these burdens that were placed upon her the moment her father surrendered her to me.

She doesn't have to live with that responsibility. All she has to do is willingly give herself to me, and she could be as free as a bird, living in a beautiful mansion with all the riches in the world and anything she could ever wish for.

"Just let it go, Charlotte. Let me love you," I whisper,

parting her legs with my hands. Her eyes close, and her head tilts back a bit as I press kisses all over her chest. Her body lights up underneath my lips. "Let me give you what you need."

My hand travels up her body, sliding underneath her dress to cup her naked breasts. With my index finger and thumb, I pinch her nipple until it's taut and her face tightens with excitement. I can't stop myself from touching her body and seeing her writhe. It feels too good, and she looks so goddamn appetizing in that dress that I almost want to take a bite.

But I have to be gentle with her for now. She's only just opening up to the idea of me fondling her, and pushing her until she withdraws is the last thing I want. No, I have to take it slow ... easy ... make her body fall for my touch before her mind does. I want her numb with emotions and sensations, and I want those delicious moans to be the only sound from her mouth.

When I hear the first one, my ears perk up, and I groan back in delight. My cock tents in my pants, but I won't pay any attention to it as I want this to be all about her. There's plenty of time to satisfy me later. First, I'll show her what she could have.

I rub her pussy through the fabric of her dress until her panties are wet. Her lips part but only moans roll off her tongue. She never opens her eyes, and I don't blame her. If she saw how she was behaving right now, it'd probably mortify her. But she needs to learn to shut off that voice in her head telling her it's wrong. Even if it is, she shouldn't care when it feels good. And I will definitely make it feel good.

She's close, so damn close, only a little further. Her cheeks are red, and droplets of sweat glisten on her skin. My tongue dips out to lick them up while I touch her and she completely unravels.

"Come for me, princess," I murmur into her ear.

She can't resist, can't fight the temptation to let go, and the explosion that follows is pure magic. Her body quivers with delicious shocks as she comes undone. I can feel it between her legs as everything tightens and her wetness grows, and the moan that rolls off her tongue sets me off.

Without thinking, I press my lips to hers and claim her mouth.

She tastes deliciously sweet and sinfully good, and I can't get enough of her lips. I want to kiss them forever, on every single fucking day because they are mine, just like the rest of her.

But then she pushes me off her and stares at me with complete indignation. As if she wasn't just as complicit in this.

Tears well up in her eyes, but she holds them back. I bring my hand to her cheeks and softly caress her.

"Why?" she mutters, her voice sounding as though she's been wiped off the earth.

And I smile in response. "Why? Because I can. That's why."

Right then, the car stops, and I open the door. "We're here."

***

Charlotte

Easton gets out of the car, leaving me on my own in this hot as fuck car as my mind reels from what just happened. From what I let him do. Why? Why did I let him overtake me like that?

The moment he started touching me, I should've stopped him. But my mouth refused to speak the words, and my body froze in place as he started to caress me. It felt as though I was under a spell, and I couldn't resist.

The temptation was too great. He knows what buttons to push to make me squirm, and he loves it. He loves the control he can exert over my body, and it makes me so damn angry. I can't tell whether I'm more upset at him for doing what he did or more upset at myself for letting him, for giving in to the moment … for coming under his command.

I can still feel his fingers all over my thighs, my breasts … my pussy. It's still thumping underneath my dress. Fuck.

When he opens the door, it takes me a few seconds to catch my breath, and from the wretched smile on his face, I know he finds it amusing. I should step out of my shoes and smack him in the head with one. Except for the moment I step outside, all thoughts of punishing him for what he just did go out the window.

I suddenly feel cold to the bone, and that's not because of the wind blowing underneath my dress.

We're right in front of a giant building that's part hotel, part restaurant.

One of my *father's* restaurants. Right here in the Netherlands.

TWENTY-TWO

Charlotte

"What the …?" I murmur, but my voice is stolen halfway through.

Banners with bold text about some grand re-opening along with my brother's name are slapped onto every decoration adorning the building.

My throat turns dry as a bone.

Easton's hand wraps around my shoulders, pulling me close to him and forcing me to walk when he does. "C'mon. Let's go inside. I'm dying to show you."

Show me … my father's renewed and renovated

restaurant, now under my brother's wing. And to show me off to them as a submissive, controllable, happy wife.

What. A. Lie.

All this time, I thought he was taking me out to dinner or to some fancy museum. But he had this planned all along. I feel cheated, used ... betrayed. As though he dangled a carrot in front of me and then ate it too, all while gazing at me.

He's cruel and unforgiving, and walking next to him up the stairs to the five-star restaurant feels like a joke. The idea of stomping on his feet and running off briefly flutters into my mind, but then I spot two guards walking behind us, who apparently drove along with us all the way to this place, and I change my mind.

We walk inside, into what's now on of my brother's hotel-restaurants, and I don't even recognize the place. A chic black and white design with lots of contrast—opposite of the warm colors my father often preferred—replace the old, overdone red and gold interior.

But I guess this is the price he had to pay to keep everything running. Not only did he need to sacrifice me for the money but he also had to change his entire business into something that didn't remotely feel like anything he'd create. Suits him well for trying to trade me. I hope the whole endeavor sinks into the ground.

Just as I hope Easton falls into a pile of shit on the way out of this restaurant should we ever leave this place. I'm pissed and at a loss for words as we stroll into the restaurant like all the other regular couples sipping drinks at the bar and chatting with each other. As if this is the normal thing to do for a rich, upper-class husband and wife. A husband who *bought* his wife from the very man he's now walking up to with a big smile on his face.

"Good afternoon, Mr. Davis," Easton says with a certain sneer.

When my father turns around to face us, I'm mortified. In an instant, our eyes connect, and the contentment evaporates from his face, making place for a grim scowl. Then he looks at Easton.

"Easton," he mumbles.

Easton holds out his hand, and my father takes it, only to be roughed up visibly. It's as though the two compete for who has the toughest handshake, and neither of them wants to give in.

"Didn't know you'd be coming too," my father says when they settle on a truce.

Easton cracks a vicious smile. "Of course. Wouldn't want to miss the grand re-opening of my latest investment here in the Netherlands … with my latest prize." He pulls me toward him for a forced hug, squeezing my ass while my father watches.

I want to spit in his face.

"Hmm, I see you two are getting along quite well," my father muses.

That's the first thing he says? No apology for selling me to this man as some kind of sacrificial lamb for his own sins? No sorry for not even contacting me and asking how I've been all this time?

Both their faces should be spat on.

"She's adjusting well in my mansion. Very easygoing and frisky, if I might say so myself," Easton retorts, and my cheeks light up like a cigarette's bud at the sight of my father's enlarged pupils.

His heart probably jumped through hoops there. And it's all because of Easton's lying ass. He should be ashamed of himself, but the moment I part my lips, Easton immediately holds up his finger right in front of my face.

"No need, Charlotte. You know how that would look on your father, right?" He glances at me from the sidelines, but it's enough to shut me up before I even begin talking. The glimmer in his eyes predicts thunder as though he's warning me not to step across the boundaries he's laying out right now.

None of this was for me. This outing wasn't for my enjoyment. I wasn't even the reason he wanted to be here. This was all because of my father and the re-opening of this restaurant. He wants to flaunt me to my family as some goddamn trophy wife. And I went along with it like a fool.

Sighing, I turn my head and gaze at all the people talking amongst one another. They're blissfully unaware of what's happened here, of all the reasons why this restaurant underwent a makeover and changed its name. Why I'm even here ... as a groomed kitty cat on a leash.

"Charlotte, why don't you go to the bar? Have a drink

and enjoy yourself," Easton says, and he leans in to press a soft but forceful kiss on my cheeks as though to show to my father I've adjusted to the situation. As though I've truly become the wife Easton's always wished for, and my father should be jealous of him.

Fuck him and fuck my father for believing his lies.

I'm not okay, and I will never pretend to be.

So I shrug Easton off and walk away without even acknowledging what either of them said. I never greeted my father, but I don't care anymore. He can drop dead for all I care. He didn't even ask if I was okay. All he cared about was what Easton said; as if it completely tilts him off his axis that he's here. Not me, his daughter, but *Easton*.

I sit on a stool at the bar and order a tequila on the rocks from the bartender. I'll need a drink or two to get through this. The question is, do I want to?

I look around the room for a moment. There are three potential exits, and only two guards following me. Sure, they're not right beside me, but they're creeping around the room, keeping their eyes on me. Easton must've paid them well, too, in case I attempt to escape.

The bartender hands me my drink, and I take a big sip. The burn feels nice going down my throat, and the sharpness takes the edge off things. I wonder how many it'd take for me to get drunk. I've never had nearly enough to get there, but tonight, I might.

As I chug down my drink, someone slides onto the stool beside me and stares at me awkwardly. A familiar smile from when I was still a youngster makes me melancholic.

"Hey, sis."

"Elijah," I mutter, putting down my glass.

"What are you doing here?" I ask, confused.

"You didn't see? My name's outside on the board." He chuckles as if it's no big deal even though it is.

"No, I mean, why are you here … at the bar? Aren't you supposed to be entertaining guests?"

"Yeah, but I figured I'd take a break and talk to my sister for once," he says.

I make a face and nod a couple of times before taking another sip.

"How are you holding up?" he asks after an awkward silence.

"How am I holding up?" I gaze at him for a second to see if he's joking, but he seems dead serious. "Well, let's see, I'm being held against my will in a mansion that's more like a prison, I was forced to marry someone I don't love, and now I'm at a place where freedom is flaunted in my face, but I'm not allowed to have it." I cock my head and make a face. "How are *you* doing?"

A smile forms on his face, but it disappears in the blink of an eye. "That sounds … rough."

I snort and take another sip of my drink. "That's not even the half of it."

He grabs my hand. "Look, I just wanted to say sorry."

"Why?" I raise a brow. "You didn't do shit." I mean it when I say that. He didn't cause this, but he also did nothing to stop it from happening either. He just sat there at my wedding and pretended nothing was wrong.

"Did you know Father exchanged me for money? The same money that bought your prized position as CEO?" I ask through gritted teeth.

His lip twitches as he swallows. "Yes, but—"

I hold my hand up right in front of his face. "I don't wanna hear it." And I take the last sip of my drink. Fuck. I'm gonna need to order a new one. There's no way I've had enough alcohol to make it through this event.

"I'm sorry, I really am," he says. "I didn't know what to do. It didn't matter what I said; Father didn't stop. He didn't want to stop."

"You could've *not* accepted the position," I retort.

"And then what? You'd still be in Mr. Van Buren's hands," he replies. "Besides, this was planned months ago. You know that."

"You could've still refused. At least you would've been an actual brother for once," I hiss back, and I signal the bartender. "Another tequila, please."

"Are you here just to drink?" he asks.

"I'm forced to be here, so I might as well drink until I don't remember any of it."

He frowns. "Forced?"

"I don't get a say in anything as a wife to that devil," I say, swallowing away all the other words I want to spout about him.

He gulps. "So it wasn't your idea to come here then?"

I make a face. "No, why would it be? Do you think I enjoy seeing people have fun because of my misery?"

His eyes narrow. "But how did Van Buren know about this event?"

"You're joking, right?" I laugh. "You're the one who's hosting this party with Father. You invited him."

"We didn't," he answers.

I pause and lower my drink for a moment. "But how did he …?"

"I don't know, but I promise you, it didn't come from us," he says.

If my father and brother didn't invite Easton, then who did? How did he know they were hosting this party at this restaurant? How did he find out that my brother's CEO appointment was today?

"It wasn't in the newspaper?" I ask.

"No. It's all hush-hush. Private invitation only."

I stare at my drink, clenching the glass, but the longer I stare, the more diluted everything seems. I feel lightheaded, sickly even, but not because of the alcohol …

Easton knew this event was happening for some reason, and the fact I can't figure out why makes me queasy.

"We did send you an invite," Elijah adds.

I gaze at him while lurking over my glass. "Where?"

"Your email. I thought you may still read it while being … *there*. You know."

He can't even say it out loud because, deep down, he knows it's wrong. And still, he won't act.

"You're a lousy brother, you know that?" I say, taking a sip of my freshly made drink.

He sucks on his top lip. "I try my best."

I snort and shake my head. "Typical. You were always Father's favorite."

"Someone had to be," he says. "I'm sorry, Charlotte, but you know how Father is. It was his way or the highway."

"Exactly why I'm in this situation as a mail-order bride." I stare off at the wall in front of me that has racks filled with bottles of liquor on them, and I wonder which one I'm going to take next.

"Hey, you could've just ... let him and his business sink, you know," Elijah says.

"And then what?" I eye him. "You wouldn't have had your shot at being CEO, and Father would be dead."

"Dead?" Elijah looks at me as though I've lost my mind.

"Oh, he hasn't told you?" I muse, sipping my drink. "Father couldn't repay the debt he owed Easton, so it was me or his life. And he chose me." I put my drink down. "Now you know."

Elijah stares in disbelief, his mouth wide open. "Father exchanged you to save his own life?" His face turns a little bit red, and he adjusts his tie and clears his throat. "Why did you accept it?"

"What else was I supposed to do? Let him die?" I know I sound like a bitch, but he's making me wanna pull my hair out.

"Well ... yeah," he says, shrugging, and I laugh.

"Typical," I say, shaking my head again. "No wonder he made you CEO. You're as heartless as he is."

He nods a couple of times and sighs. "I guess I deserve that."

"You do, yeah," I reply cynically.

"Look." He places a hand on my arm. "I wanna help you. Tell me what I can do."

"What can you do, Elijah? If I don't stay with Easton, he'll have Father murdered."

"Why do you care so much?" he asks.

"He's our father; how could I not?"

He sucks on his bottom lip again almost as if he can't believe what I'm saying. Maybe I have more of our mother inside me than I thought. I don't remember much about her, but I do remember she was always kind to people. And she genuinely loved and cared for us, unlike our father. Too bad I didn't get a lot of time with her. Cancer's a bitch.

"Well, whatever the case, if you need my help for whatever reason"—Elijah leans forward and winks—"you know you can always come to me, right?"

I soak up his words and cock my head at him. "You think I can get out of that house? That I have access to a phone, the internet, basic things?" I laugh. "You really have no idea, do you?"

He looks befuddled.

"I'm a prisoner, Elijah. I'm not free to do whatever I want. I have no way of contacting anyone on the outside world," I say, clenching my drink as though it's my lifeline.

"In fact, this is the first time I've been outside the property's fences since we got married."

He grimaces. "Does he hurt you?"

"No ... not physically," I say.

Elijah squeezes my arm. "Tell me."

"It's ..." How can I tell him? How can I explain to my brother what it's like to be a woman? To be wanted for your body but not your brain? To be used like a sex doll and thrown aside like an old toy?

I can't. Not when my father's life and Elijah's position as CEO are at stake. Despite the fact that my father doesn't give a damn about me ... I can't let him die. That's not who I am.

"It's nothing," I say.

"You're lying. I know when you're lying, Charlotte. You did it all the time when we were young."

"You don't understand," I snap. "I never had anyone before. He's my first. My first ever ... the man who's keeping me as a pet." Tears well up in my eyes, and I fight to keep them at bay.

Elijah grabs a few strands of my hair and tucks them behind my ear, and his gentle touch has a single tear rolling down my cheek, which I wipe away with the back of my hand.

"You're right, I don't. But I know you're strong, and you can do anything you set your mind to."

His words feel rehearsed, just as I've come to expect from the man who has to follow in my father's footsteps.

It's only natural for them to feel less and less over time. After all, emotions only hold you back and keep you from true power.

I turn my head and close my eyes, breathing out a sigh.

"It was nice speaking with you, Elijah," I say. "Go entertain your guests."

He nods. I'm sure he understands there's nothing more we can do for each other. No one can destroy Easton's desire to claim me as his own, not even my brother. And as long as Easton remains their biggest investor, there's no way Elijah would risk hurting or even killing him. Sacrificing his spot as CEO to save me from this life is too much to ask of him.

Even though he's my brother, even though people always say family goes above all else ... my family values money above all else, and nothing will ever change that.

"In any case, I'm going to investigate how Easton knew about this event. Maybe he's been digging into our family business," Elijah mutters.

He gets off his stool, but before he goes, he orders another drink for me and scoots it over to me. Then he says, "Make sure you enjoy this ... as long as it lasts." He adds a tentative smile before leaving me behind at the bar. The smile on his face grows when he spots familiar people, probably others our father introduced him to for the sake of the company. Everything is for the sake of the company and our legacy as a family, including his fake smile that appears and vanishes as quickly as his heart does.

As I grab the glass and stare at the contents, I notice the camera hanging in the back of the room. It immediately reminds me of all the cameras in Easton's house, and how he's always aware of where I am. And it makes me question … where else does he watch people? How do I know it's contained to his house only? What if …

The glass in my hand topples over, and I stare in disbelief at the alcohol pouring over the bar. The bartender jumps into action, wiping it all up.

"Sorry," I mutter, frozen in place.

"It's fine," he replies, swiftly cleaning the bar and leaving it as shiny as it was before I knocked over my glass.

I didn't mean to, but something made me snap. A memory of a night from before I was married when I was still in my own bed in my own home …

And found the main door unlocked the morning after I woke up even though I was a thousand percent sure I locked myself inside.

Fear ripples across my back.

What if it was *him*?

TWENTY-THREE

EASTON

On our way home, Charlotte's unusually quiet. When I found her at the bar, she was staring off into space with hollow eyes and cold fingers. She came without a fuss, not even a word. In fact, I don't think she's spoken to me at all since we arrived at the restaurant.

I suppose seeing her father and brother alive and happy was a bit of a shock to her. It's one of the reasons I decided to attend the event uninvited. Of course, her father didn't expect to see me there, but I always need to make sure my investments are solid. I wouldn't want my name attached to any failing business.

Charlotte was probably dying to see her brother, so I

gave her some time alone at the restaurant to spend however she chose. I'd hoped it would take the edge off things. After all, it's time outside the mansion, time which she highly values. I didn't expect her to end up this ... shaken. Maybe I misjudged her coping abilities. Unless her brother said something to her that caused her to break.

I pull her closer toward me in the car, but she only petrifies. "Did you have a good time?" I ask in an attempt to lift her mood.

"No," she replies, and she tries to shake me off. "If that's your version of a date, I don't want to go on any more dates."

"No." I laugh, but she's not even slightly amused. "But I thought you'd enjoy seeing your family."

"They're *not* my family," she huffs. "Not anymore."

"Well, I'm glad you see it that way." I smile at her.

She gives me the stink eye. "Neither are you. I don't need any family."

"Everybody needs family. And I need you," I say, and I caress her cheek, but she leans away from me. "What's gotten into you? I took you outside and off the property. I gave you what you wished for."

"No, you gave yourself what you wanted, which was seeing my father's face and pride dissolve when he saw me."

Well, I did enjoy showing off my prize and seeing how badly his business was going, but I didn't bring her there just for that, so I shake my head. "Nonsense. He doesn't care about that."

"About me?" she retorts, raising a brow.

I grab her chin and make her look at me. "He doesn't give a shit that I took you. *That's* how much he loved you."

She jerks free from my grip. "Like you're any better."

"At least I try to be," I retort.

"You *bought* me," she quips.

"*He* sold you," I hiss.

"Semantics," she replies, side-eyeing me. "How long are we gonna play this game?"

"As long as you can keep it up." Or as long as I have the patience to deal with her.

"What do you want from me?" she asks. "Do you want me to be grateful for the chance to spend time with you at my father's business while my brother ascends the throne over my rotting corpse?"

"Is that what you think happened to you? You equate being in my care to a rotting corpse?" I have to admit I'm a bit offended by that remark. My house is not a graveyard.

"Might as well since we're both dead inside," she huffs, crossing her arms.

"You're only saying that because you're upset," I reply.

"Because you dangled a carrot in front of me and it. Was. A. Lie." She pronounces each word as though it's her last.

I cock my head at her. "You're assuming this was the only time I'll ever take you out," I say. "Keep going like that, and it might become reality."

She huffs. "So what, it was a test?"

I clear my throat. "Perhaps."

I wanted to see what she'd do. I even brought along a few guards to make sure she wouldn't get away should she attempt to escape. But also to protect both me and her should anything happen to her. Maybe someone would try to steal her away from me again, so I wanted to prevent that at all costs.

But she surprised me by staying at the bar. She didn't even try to run, which is commendable. Maybe there is some hope left after all.

"I'm proud of you," I say, leaning toward her. "You faced your family with dignity and didn't give in to their needs."

"No ... but I gave in to yours," she says, sighing.

"And there's absolutely nothing wrong with that," I whisper, placing a hand on her thigh. "There's nothing wrong with letting go in the moment, Charlotte. You're allowed to enjoy every touch, every kiss ... every bit of my ownership."

She sucks in a breath as I reach up toward that same spot as before. "I can do this every time we go out as a reward for your patience."

The moment I touch her pussy, she murmurs, "Stop."

I pause and allow her to breathe for a moment.

She gazes at me from underneath those eyelashes with those beautiful, soul-sucking eyes that could make any man's knees buckle under their weight. "Can we go home? Please?"

The word *home* punctures my heart. Finally, she views my house as her home.

Despite the fact she hated seeing her family, we've made some progress here. Maybe she learned I'm not the worst person to be with, and that I'll give her more freedom if she behaves.

But I know she's upset, and I don't like to see her that way. Even though I'm an asshole, I have a heart too hidden somewhere deep inside. And it's turning softer and softer the more time I spend with her.

"Of course, princess." I smile and lift my hand to grab hers and then kiss the top. "But first, there's something else I have to do."

Her brows furrow. "Where?"

A smirk appears on my lips. "You'll see."

***

Charlotte

He's so elusive all the time, and I can't get through to him, no matter how many questions I ask. It's like he doesn't want me to get close or to understand him. As if he's deliberately keeping me at bay.

It's not working. I can see right through him, just as I saw right through that whole façade back at my brother's restaurant. Where we're going is a mystery, but it must be another ploy to get me on my knees or make me cry. Either way, I don't trust him.

The car drives through town, and I watch the people outside from my little cocoon inside, like a doll in her little dollhouse looking out into the world she can't have.

I sigh. "How long will it take?"

"We're almost there," Easton answers. Instead of a vicious grin, there's now a modest but genuine smile on his face, but he quickly looks away as though he doesn't want me to see.

Whatever, I'm so done with today. After that game he just played, I feel like a fool for even thinking he could ever care about anyone but himself.

When the car stops, Easton gets out first and walks to my side, opening up my door like a true gentleman would, but it's only for show. He's done it many times before, and this is no different.

Except he doesn't hook his arm around mine this time. Instead, he grabs my hand and tugs me along without pulling.

The building in front of me is an old one, but it's decorated with all kinds of colorful murals and lights. But as I try to look around, Easton's driver comes storming past with two heavy boxes.

"Excuse me!"

"No worries," Easton says. "We'll meet up inside."

"Yes, sir!" the driver says as he enters the building.

I swallow. "What is this place?"

"C'mon. I'll show you." Easton holds my hand as we go inside.

There are hallways filled with doors and kids sprouting from every nook and cranny. At the end is a big common room with a television, a few couches, some game consoles, and toys littered everywhere. There are even bookcases against the wall on the other side of the room, but there are only a few books inside.

"What ... is this?" I mutter as Easton lets go of my hand.

He goes into the main area where some of the kids gather as his driver places the boxes on a table. The driver leaves and nods at me as he passes me as a courtesy. Then a woman walks out of the kitchen area and smiles broadly at Easton.

"Oh, je bent er!" she exclaims, and she approaches him to kiss him three times on the cheeks.

"Can we talk English?" Easton mumbles, glancing toward me for a second. "She can't speak Dutch."

"Of course," the lady says. "The kids were so eager to see you. They've been talking about it all day."

"I'll bet," he replies as the kids gather all around him.

"Meneer Van Buren!" One of the kids runs toward him, wrapping his arms around his leg.

"Hey, David." Easton pets him on the head.

"Let's talk English, guys," he says. "I've brought a guest who doesn't understand Dutch." He throws me another glance, and so do all the kids, making my face heat. I try not to draw attention to myself as I watch from afar, clutching the doorpost as Easton goes to his knees.

"Now, I've brought you all some things again, but you have to promise me you'll take good care of them and treat them with respect," he says.

"What is it?" one of the other kids asks.

Easton cocks his head, and says, "Open the box. Go have a look."

The kids swarm the table and rip open the package. They can't help themselves. Book after book is pulled out of the box, and they hold it above their heads like a lost treasure they found.

And the smile on Easton's face as he watches the little kids scream and dance around with the books, some of them giving them a neat spot in the empty bookcase, is infectious. So much so that I can't stop grinning as he looks me dead in the eyes.

He sure surprised everyone here, not just the kids. There's something good in him after all.

"What do we say, kids?" the lady says.

"Thank you, Mr. Van Buren!" the kids say.

"Don't mention it," he says. "I'll be back soon with more."

One of the kids hugs his legs again, and he's having trouble shaking them off. I giggle when the last one's finally off his shoulder as he approaches me.

"What?" He lifts a brow.

I shrug. "That was nice of you to do."

"Thanks," he says.

He eyes me from the side, and I do the same to him, neither of us speaking the words we obviously want to say. It's too embarrassing to admit that for a second there I actually liked him and that I could actually see the humble, generous man behind the rough façade. The true gentleman he can be when he isn't trying to be a depraved bastard.

And I think he knows that too.

He showed me something sweet and kind ... His weak spot.

Something I could use as a weapon ... but choose not to because I won't stoop to his level. I'd rather admire the realness and keep it in my heart to remember for rocky times.

***

EASTON

When we get home, she seems anxious to get out of the car. Luckily, the door only opens from the outside, so she always has to wait until someone comes to pick her up. I open the door and take her hand as she steps out, and I take her back into my home. For the first time ever, she doesn't release my hand as we step inside the main hallway. Maybe she's warming up to me. After showing her the charity work that I do, she finally saw some humanity in me after all.

Or maybe she's learned that opposing me is futile. Whatever the case, I'm positive she's adjusting well to her new status as my wife.

She turns toward me, and says, "Can I ... look around the house a little?"

Such a strange request. I'm a bit befuddled by it.

"I haven't had the chance," she adds. "And I want to get to know my home."

How could I deny her? "Of course. You can explore as much as you like, but ..." I raise a finger. "My study is off-limits."

She nods. "I just wanna see ..." She bites her lip and glances over my shoulder at the closed door to my study.

"What?" I mutter.

"The cameras." She gazes straight into my eyes as her tongue swipes across the top of her lip, and it immediately makes my cock hard. "Where you watch me."

"Hmm ..." A lopsided grin forms on my face.

"Can I see them?" She cocks her head and continues to bite her lip in that seductive way that makes me want to pick her up and bang her against the hardwood door.

"I only wanna take a peek. That's all," she adds.

I narrow my eyes at her. When did she learn to use her attractiveness as a weapon? She sure drives a hard bargain. I like it. "As long as you don't touch anything."

Her eyes glow brightly. "I promise I won't."

I firmly grab her hand and take her toward the door, unlocking it with the key from my pocket. She walks inside and marvels at all the books. The last time we were here, she was running away from me while we were arguing. There was no time to appreciate my collection or the aesthetics of this room. It's my favorite place in the house ... after her bathroom, of course.

She inspects some of my collectibles, such as a statue that came from Egypt and an old handcrafted globe from the 1800s. Then she walks up to my desk and slides her hand along the wood as though it hides a million secrets she can't wait to unravel.

"So this is where you sit?" she asks.

"To view the cameras? Yes," I reply as I approach her from behind.

"But there's only a laptop," she says, opening it. Obviously, it's locked with a password so she can't see anything I don't want her to see. And if she ever did manage to unlock it, this laptop is stationary and has no connection to the internet, only the intranet. I don't want her sending out calls for help. Besides, I doubt she'll ever find my trusty work laptop hidden in a secret compartment in my room.

"You don't need much more than that," I muse, standing right behind her as she closes the laptop and arches her back when I place a hand on her waist. My cock presses against her ass as I whisper in her ear, "But where's the fun in that?"

She sucks in a breath while I lean forward, but instead of kissing her on the back of the neck, I press a tiny button underneath my desk. She gasps as a huge screen appears in front of us, sliding out of the top of the windowsill.

I give a voice command. "Show cameras."

The screen immediately shows about a dozen or more live feeds from several cameras around my home, along with the one situated in her bedroom and bathroom ... and the room we're currently standing in.

I don't even have to look at her to know she's impressed because I can feel her breath faltering from where my hand is resting. Her finger lifts toward the screen, pointing at that one camera filming us right now. She cocks her head and waves, then she checks the room to find the camera above the door.

"Found it," I mutter, smiling as she's spun around in my arms while she was searching.

I place both hands on the desk behind her, trapping her. Her cheeks turn red as she leans back against the desk, and there's a definite sheen of sweat right above her chest.

"Do the cameras scare you?" I ask with a low tone of voice.

She swallows and places her hands on the desk too. "No. I'm just surprised at the number."

"Do you think these are all of them?"

"No."

My smile broadens, and I grab a strand of her hair and

curl it around my finger.

Smart girl.

"Are you the only one who watches?" she asks.

"No one has access to this room except me," I reply, taking in the scent of her hair and cherishing the smell of her perfume. "So yes." The strand of hair rolls through my fingers until nothing's left but air filled with friction between us. And fuck me, is it on fire.

"How many times a day do you watch me?" she asks.

"As often as I can," I reply, and her face only turns more into the shade of a strawberry. It matches her dress nicely.

A hint of a smile tips up her lips. "Does it turn you on to watch me?"

"Oh, yes." Just the thought gets me riled up.

She grips the desk tight, her fingers digging into the wood as she bites her lip. I can tell she's waiting for me to do something, to take her right here and now … but should I? She smells like tequila, and I bet she drank too much of it, considering her flushed cheeks. But she's literally standing here with her legs opened wide, her ass leaning on my desk, chest out and nipples peaked as if she means to lure me.

With an index finger, I tip up her chin. "Are you afraid of me? Tell me the truth."

Her teeth barely separate as she says, "No." The word comes out strong and powerful, spoken like a true queen. But can I take her seriously? Or is she playing mind games with me?

One second, she didn't want anything to do with me, and the next, she's here, flaunting her body. She can't seem to make up her damn mind.

But that's just it. I wanted her in that position where she'd question her own morality, her needs, and her desires. I want her to *want* me, and now she finally does.

I can't fucking say no, so I grab her face and kiss her hard. Her mouth latches onto mine as we tug and fight while kissing, her tongue rolling around mine, trying to take control. I can taste the liquor on her tongue, but it adds a nice edge to our kiss. And fuck me, does she taste delicious.

I want more. No, I *need* more.

My hands wrap around her ass and lift her onto the desk while I kiss her as if my life depends on it. I don't intend to stop. She's far too delectable to ever let go, and she knows this. It was about time she gave in.

Suddenly, she unlocks her mouth from mine, and whispers, "Wait."

"No," I say, kissing her again, but she shoves me back.

"We can't do this," she says.

"Why?" I frown.

"Because it's fucking wrong, and you know it," she replies. "I'm drunk."

Her lips are swollen and completely wet when she says this, but I don't for one second believe she doesn't want this. Her sultry eyes give her away.

"Do I look like a man who cares?" I growl, and I plant my lips back on hers, not giving a shit what she or anyone else thinks of it.

She may be fucking delirious from the alcohol, but I don't fucking care. She tempted me, seduced me like the little vixen she is, and now she'll pay the price.

"You want this, Charlotte ... admit it," I murmur between kisses, and my tongue dips out to lick the roof of her mouth. I can't stop kissing her; her lips are driving me nuts. She's everything I ever imagined, everything I ever wanted, and I'm not letting her out of this room until I've had my way with her.

My lips are everywhere; on her lips, her chin, her neck, her collarbones, and even the top of her breasts. After one brief second to breathe, she whispers, "I hate you."

"Hate me, love me, I don't care ... but I *will* have you," I growl back, and I tear her dress, ripping apart the strings tied behind her neck. She yelps, but I cover her mouth with mine before she alerts the staff.

"Shhh ..." I murmur, narrowing my eyes. "Keep quiet or else ..."

"Or else what?" she mutters, her eyes widening.

"I'll tie you up and put a ball gag in your mouth."

"Oh, my God," she mutters.

I push her back down onto the desk, and say, "Now spread your legs like you did before."

With a face as cold as ice, she does what I ask, just like before, but this time, she kicks off her shoes too.

A smile spreads on my lips. "Expecting something?"

"You and I both know I won't get out of here before

you've had your fix," she muses.

Touché. How does she know me so well? I've barely shown myself to her, yet she can read me like a book. Such a fucking smartass. That might come back to bite me in the ass later.

But first, I wanna fucking bite hers.

TWENTY-FOUR

Charlotte

"Good thinking," Easton says with a dark, seductive voice. "Now turn around."

I frown. "Why?"

He takes off his belt, pulling it through the loops with care before snapping it on his hand. Over … and over … again. My eyes can't stop focusing on it while his sparkle with excitement at the sight of my terror.

"What are you going to do?" I mutter.

"Do what I say, princess." The harshness in his voice makes me gulp. I shouldn't mess with him right now. His muscles are tense as though he's completely ready to fuck the living shit out of me. But that's just it ... I'm not sure I'm ready.

I've never done this before. An actual dick has never been inside me. Maybe a few toys, but that was it. I already accepted he was going to be my first, but I just didn't know *when*. But now that the time has arrived, am I ready? Am I willing to do this?

I swallow away the lump in my throat while his cock grows harder and harder in his pants. A part of me wants to run for the hills, but another is eager to use this opportunity to my advantage. This is the only way ... the only way to get him to trust me ... So that I can *use* him too.

I spin on my feet and face the screen. The camera points right at us, my body on full display as he steps behind me and grabs my wrists, pinning them on my back. He ties them together tightly until the leather burns into my skin. A whimper rolls off my lips, but he covers my mouth with a hand.

"No crying, princess. All I want from you are moans," he growls.

Suddenly, a flat hand lands on my ass.

I squeak, but his hand muffles the sound.

"What did I say?"

He slaps me again, harder this time. The sound emanating from my lungs is unstoppable. The stinging sensation left on my skin heats my core, and tears sting my eyes.

"Not a single mewl," he growls, and he smacks me again, repeating it until all that's left are ragged breaths and unwanted desire pooling between my legs. My knees are weak, and my legs are close to giving in. The desk is the only thing keeping me standing.

"Good. You're finally beginning to learn," he says.

He lifts my dress all the way over my ass and rips down my panties in one go. I gasp and turn my head, but he immediately shoves my face onto the desk. "Who said you could look?"

A sudden finger up my pussy makes me moan out loud.

I didn't mean to talk. It slipped out.

His finger goes up and down, each stroke a little farther until he's inside me completely. My body reels with energy, and at the same time, I feel meek like a little lamb. I despise him, yet I can't say no, can't speak up. All I can do is lie here and accept his lust.

When he pulls out, I pant with relief. But he's far from done with me.

He continues stroking my clit, getting me all hot and bothered.

"See how much you want this? How wet you are for me?" he growls. "I *own* you. Whether you like it or not, your body belongs to me. It sings for me, Charlotte, and you will too."

Fuck, he's right, and I hate it. I fucking hate it with all my guts.

But this had to happen. After all the pushing and

pulling, the tug-of-war we had, this was the only outcome. And as he thrums my pussy and circles my clit, I'm not even sure I mind.

He plays me like a violin and knows how to make me greedy for more.

Suddenly, he pulls his fingers away, and my head spins with unfulfilled desire.

Without warning, he inserts his finger into my ass.

I squeal, and he slaps me again, causing intense pulsations all across my body.

Fuck. This feels so wrong. So ... immoral.

It's exactly the way he wants me to feel. How he likes it.

Dirty. Bad. Nasty.

But the more he twists and turns, thrusting and fucking me with his finger, the more my body zings. I shouldn't want this, shouldn't even enjoy this ... whatever it is he's going to do.

"Hmm, you're so willing tonight. I can't wait to use those pretty fuck holes of yours," he murmurs, groaning in delight.

He pulls out again, and I feel empty. As though my brain malfunctioned and his fingering pulled the plug.

My eyes can't help but glance over my shoulder, and I instantly regret it. He's fished something out of a locked drawer ... lube, and a black, cone-shaped silicone object with a diamond at the end. My eyes widen.

"Is that ...?"

SMACK!

Another slap on my ass has me moaning, and I buck against the table.

"I didn't say you could look, and I never said you could speak," he says, and I can hear him squirt lube onto the object. "You need to learn to behave, princess. Maybe this will bring you to your knees."

Before I know it, he's spread my cheeks and pushes something against my ass.

"Don't fight it. It'll only hurt more," he growls as he pushes the object in.

"What is it?" I squeal.

"A butt plug," he replies.

Oh my God. A butt plug? Fuck. Those are used in porn. Not ... real life. Right?

He's inserting it. Everything stretches, burns, and pinches as though it doesn't fit. And my pussy clenches and tightens each time he pushes. The final plop puts the plug into place, and my ass feels fuller than it's ever felt before.

Fuck. The sensations almost made me come right there and then.

"Good girl," Easton says.

When he slaps my ass again, my whole body pulses with arousal, and it's unlike anything I've ever felt before. His hand caresses my cheeks, softly sliding along my curves until he reaches my pussy. Right before he touches me, he stops, leaving me with an indescribable wantonness that stirs the soul.

He scoots his desk chair closer and plops down onto it

right behind me. He's watching me, I just know it, and my cheeks heat from the thought. When he groans out loud, my clit thumps with pleasure.

The chair screeches a little as it slides closer ... and closer ... and closer.

A sudden warm breath on my pussy has me arching my back.

"Stay ... still," he murmurs, his face hovering mere inches from my pussy.

The moment his tongue touches my skin, I'm lost. Lost to his mouth and the way he circles that tongue all around my clit. Goose bumps scatter on my skin as he kisses and sucks me. His soft lips are pleasurable on my clit, and he knows just how to lick me to make me squirm.

This was his plan all along. To make me angry with my family so that I'd give in to his demands. And it's working so well that I don't even know anymore whether this sexual encounter was my idea or his.

All the lines blur as he sticks his tongue into my pussy. My mind is numb with pleasure, and I can't think anymore. I had a plan, but that's gone out the window too with him tying my wrists on my back. All I can do is enjoy while being at his mercy.

And fuck me ... does it feel right.

"So fucking wet for me." Easton groans, alternating his licking and sucking until I've gone mad with lust. "Come for me, princess. Show me how much you like this."

I feel humiliated. Used. Planted on a desk with my ass in

the air and every inch of my body on display. The cameras are recording this as we speak. Who else will see them? And did he lock the doors? God, I hope no one comes in.

"Stop thinking," Easton growls. "I know you're holding back."

"How?" I mutter.

He slaps me once more, but I've gotten used to the stinging pain of his flat hand. Then he bites my ass cheek.

"Ow! What did you do that for?" I say.

"Because you're clenching your legs. Spread 'em." He nudges them apart and forces me to spread wide. But the more I do, the more I'm shaking on my feet.

"Yes ... release all that pleasure, Charlotte. You know you want to," he murmurs against my skin.

I'm lost in delirium. Drowning in my own lust and spiraling out of control.

And as he presses his tongue onto my clit, I come. Right then, he smacks my ass and pushes a finger into my pussy. The wave of ecstasy that follows has my body clenching around his finger. The pulses are so heavy and so uncontrollable that my knees buckle under me. But Easton captures me in his arms and forces me to stay upright while he finishes the job.

When he's done, I'm still lying face down on the desk, completely wiped out.

What will he do now? Will he take me for himself?

I'm expecting him to zip down and claim me at any moment now.

Instead, he stops touching me and sits back in his chair.

I turn my head toward him. His pants are undone with his giant cock on full display. The size still makes me gulp. I can't believe that's been in my mouth.

But the longer I stare, the more impatient I'm getting. I was ready, albeit unwilling, but able to do this so I could get under his skin and gain the upper hand. What's going on?

"Aren't you going to …?"

"What?" He raises a brow. "Fuck you?"

Those two words sound so fucking sinful from his mouth.

The devilish grin on his face makes me weak and enraged at the same time.

The next word breaks me completely.

"No."

***

EASTON

Finally, I have her right where I want her.

On my desk, spread for my joy, naked.

It's exactly how I imagined this would go, how I fantasized about it years ago, yet I'm not going to go all the way. I'm not going to claim her pussy as mine. I'm not going to steal her cherry and be her first time. Not now … not when she's half-drunk and completely wiped out.

No, I want her begging for it.

I want her to scream my name and plead for me to fill her pussy with my cum.

Then, and only then, will I mark her as mine.

"You'll have to beg me for it," I growl, touching myself as she stands there against the desk with all her beautiful holes in full view. God, I can't wait to fucking fill them up. But she needs to submit to me first.

All of this was just a step on the grand stairs toward being my pet. My princess needs to learn what it means to truly give in. But she'll get there eventually. It's only a matter of time.

So I rub myself while she stares at me over her shoulder. I don't give a damn what she thinks. I'm still going to come all over her.

I slap her ass again for good measure. "I didn't say you could turn around."

"But you—"

"I'm doing what I desire. Now stay there and spread your legs, princess. Show me those beautiful fuck holes of yours."

Her whole body blushes along when she hears the words. I know she hates it when I talk about her as though she's just a doll I could fuck. And I want her to feel that way so she'll remember who's in charge.

She will not manipulate me into doing what she wants. I'm in control.

I love it when she submits ... And I love what I'm seeing in front of me. That beautiful diamond inside her ass sparkles with each tiny movement she makes, and it turns me on so much that I've decided here and now I'm going to come all over her ass.

With fury, I jerk myself off to the pretty girl standing right in front of me whose legs are still shaking from what I did. I bet she liked my tongue all up in her pussy even though she'll probably yell at me later for doing just that. She can't handle her desire ... yet. But I know just how to silence the noise inside her mind. Shut it off. A tiny whack is all that's required to reset her. The pain is a nice bonus.

I smack her ass once more, just for fun, because it turns me on. I admit, I'm a bastard, but I don't fucking care. She's my wife, and I can do whatever the hell I want. And right now, what I want is her pleasing the fuck out of me.

"Keep those tits on the desk," I growl. "Don't fucking move."

Her shoulders rise each time she breathes. They're shallow breaths, and she huffs with each one of them as though she's trying to keep her shit together. It's the first time in ages she doesn't tell me off or shout at me or swear. I guess she's learning. Good.

My eyes hone in on that sweet, delectable pussy of hers. Fuck, she tasted divine, and I can't wait to dig in again. But not tonight ... No, I want her to soak in the pleasure I gave her. I want her to fucking bathe in it so she'll remember it always.

Even if she doesn't like it, I own her body.

My tongue's been there.

I licked it, so it's mine.

And with that thought, I come hard, all over her round, perky ass and the jewel that adorns it.

A groan escapes my mouth as I release all my pent-up energy. When the orgasm subsides, I admire the creamy substance splattered all over her like a picturesque painting.

A devious smile forms on my lips. Oh, I'll have so much fucking fun re-watching the video that the camera above us just made.

Zipping myself up, I rise out of the chair and pull the plug from her ass, placing it on the desk so that I can clean it later. She lets out an exasperated sigh as I take the belt off her wrists and flip her around in my arms. Her eyes are glassy as though she's not really here.

I cup her face and bring her closer, pressing a soft kiss onto her lips.

"Now you know what you taste like …" I mutter.

She places a hand on my waist, and purrs, "Sweet and sour …"

"Perfect," I add. "Just like you."

She lifts her dress over her tits again, barely masking the fact that I completely ripped it apart. "Hmm … You're trying to seduce me."

"Is it working?" I jest, raising a brow.

"No," she says, trying to maintain a straight face.

"Right … keep telling yourself that," I say.

She takes in a deep breath through her nose but doesn't reply. Good. She's learning fast.

"Are you done?" she asks.

Of course, she makes it seem as though this was all for me. Like it was my idea, my choice.

It wasn't.

But if she feels better to think that, then I'll accept that.

One last peck on her cheeks, and I whisper into her ear, "Good night, Charlotte. Sleep well."

She narrows her eyes and then releases my waist, walking off into the hallway with her torn dress as though nothing ever happened. But we both know *something* did.

And that something was her body … tethering to mine.

***

Charlotte

In my room, I immediately undress.

A key drops to the floor.

A key I'd hidden between my body and the fabric.

A key … I snatched right out of his pocket when he wasn't paying attention.

I can't help but grin as I pick it up from the floor and

stare at it. All that dirty, raunchy sex was worth it to get my hands on this treasure. Even the fact that my ass hurts doesn't compare to the gleeful excitement in my heart. This key opens the secret drawer in his study, the one place he actively kept me away from.

He's desperately trying to keep something hidden, and I wanna find out what it is. After all, husbands and wives shouldn't keep secrets from each other. And this wife will be researching of her own volition without her husband's knowledge. Because she too can play that game.

TWENTY-FIVE

Charlotte

Without even glancing at the camera hanging above me, I go to bed naked and pretend to fall asleep with the key clutched firmly between my fingers. There, I wait for hours, checking the clock every once in a while when I turn around.

Once the clock reaches 3:00 a.m., I slide out of bed and put on a bathrobe. I walk out of my room and close the door softly so as not to disturb anyone. No one appears to be in the house, though I reckon guards will be waiting outside should I try to escape.

But I won't … I'm only going on a short exploration, and I know just where to go. On my toes, I slip downstairs and to his study. The door's locked, so I pull out my key and wriggle it into the lock, twisting it. A soft click follows, and the door opens.

My heart pounds in my throat as I go inside and close the door behind me, then move straight to his desk. No one's here, so I'm sure he's gone to bed as I'm sure his favorite pastime is watching me lose my mind in my room. He sits here every single day, doing whatever it is that he does to make more money and get more power. And I know for sure this key leads to something right here in this very room.

My hand slides along the surface of the desk, below the rim, searching for a button. *Got it.* The screen comes down again, showing the live video feed. Unsurprisingly, no cameras are inside his room. He only spies on others, but no one can spy on him. Filthy, dirty bastard with his filthy, dirty fingers touching me in places I haven't even been. And it was right here against this desk …

Just touching the wood makes me feel his fingers inside me again, toying with me, playing with my clit while he kisses me on the lips, and for some reason, it instantly makes me clench my legs together.

No, I can't think about that. Not now, not ever.

I open the laptop on the desk and turn it on. It's password protected, but that won't stop me from trying, so I enter a bunch of random things that come to mind.

VanBuren.

Error.

CharlotteDavis.

Error.

Only one more try left. Shit. Hmm ... what about ...

CharlotteVanBuren.

Ping.

The laptop switches on, and I'm left with a lopsided grin on my face. That asshole made *my name* his password? I'm not even surprised even though it's creepy. It's Easton Van Buren, after all.

I check his laptop files and try to find something about myself using the search option but to no avail. There's no information about me on this thing except for the video files maybe. So I open those and press the timestamp for yesterday evening.

Our sexcapade was definitely caught on camera. In fact, my pussy is in full view and so is his dick as he strokes it. My cheeks heat again, and I gulp from the way he shoves that plug into my ass.

I close the file before I get all hot and bothered again. He has folders filled to the brim with videos such as these. What does he plan to do with them? Use them to jerk off to? Extort me with them?

Whatever the case, I can't let it happen, so I immediately move all the files from last night into the bin and permanently delete them from his computer with a smirk on my face. I turn off the camera in this room for an hour so it won't record me being in here, and I've also erased the footage it already took.

That'll teach him not to mess with me.

But I shouldn't forget why I came here in the first place; the entire reason I got myself in this situation so I could steal his key. He must be keeping something more from me because he knew my father and brother were having that celebration at the restaurant. I need to find out how.

I search his laptop through, leaving nothing uncovered. However, there's little to nothing on this laptop about his business. Everything's locked behind passwords, and no matter how many times I guess, I can't figure it out, and it's infuriating. For some reason, it also has no access to the internet either, which means I can't send out an email or any other call for help.

I sigh out loud and lean against the desk, wondering if it was all for nothing.

That's when my fingers slide along the locked drawer.

What if ...

I immediately go to my knees and touch the lock. It looks the same as the one in the door, so I grab my key and push it in, twisting it. A click follows, and my heart jumps into my throat. I pull open the drawer and look around to make sure no one's watching before I peer inside.

On the bottom lies a notebook ... pink ... fluffy ...

Mine.

My eyes widen, and my breathing falters as I pick up the notebook I used as both a diary and a planner. I sink to the floor with the fluffy pink notebook in my hands. I'm shaking as I open it and read my own handwritten notes on the pages. My heart races, and my stomach twists as I sift through the pages finding that one date ... the date my father's company would be given to my brother.

It's all in here. This is where he found out about the party at that restaurant.

From *my* notebook.

That I *never* gave to him.

In fact, I've never even carried it outside my little apartment.

My fingers tremble at the sight of the words.

Easton had this in his possession all this time. My notebook ... stolen from my apartment. The same notebook that suddenly vanished a couple of months ago even though I turned my whole apartment upside down looking for it.

Easton's been in my apartment, and he took something away from me without my knowledge. Without my permission.

Shivers run up and down my spine at the thought of him coming into my apartment when I wasn't even there ... or, worse, when I was.

Because there was this one night when I woke in the middle of what felt like a dream, when someone touched my face and hair, and a draft entered my room. What if it wasn't a dream after all? What if it was ... *him*?

What if he was there all along, watching me ... stalking

me?

My entire body feels numb and cold to the bone as I scramble off the floor with that notebook still in my hand.

No wonder he knows so much about me, about what I like, my style, my favorites, my dislikes. It's all in here. This fucking notebook gave away my life. And he used it against me.

Tears well up in my eyes. I want to shred this thing to pieces. Rip it apart and chuck it out the window. But if I did that, I'd give myself away.

He'd know I'd been to his study alone, and that I'd meddled with his affairs. He'd know I'd stolen a key that belongs to him.

And he'd probably punish me for it.

Hell, I'd be surprised if he didn't lock me up in my room for the rest of my life.

There's no other choice. I should put the notebook back where I found it.

My fingers reach for the drawer, and I stare at the wood as though it's a coffin where I'm about to leave my beloved friend. If Easton keeps this in his possession, he'll be able to use all my own thoughts and wishes against me all over.

Could I? Would I be able to live with that?

Suddenly, a clicking noise has me on edge, and I shut the drawer and duck for cover.

Someone walks past the room, a light emanating from the hallway. Luckily, they don't come inside and go up the stairs instead.

But I can't calm myself. What if they come back? I have to get out of here before someone finds me in here, so I close the laptop, lock everything up again, and leave the room exactly the way it was.

Except for the notebook.

Because that notebook belongs to *me*. Not him.

And no one else but me will keep it hidden.

TWENTY-SIX

EASTON

In the morning, I wait for her at breakfast as I always do. I prefer my days to start with plenty of coffee, a newspaper, and some light banter. It cheers me up a lot, especially when it's chatter with her. For some reason, I can't get enough of her filthy mouth even though she uses it to throw all kinds of expletives in my face. I don't mind because I adore her tenacity.

It's a shame she refuses to talk to me this morning. In fact, from the moment she walked in, she seems as pale as a ghost, and I can't help but wonder if it's because of what we did in my study. Or rather … all the debauchery I put her through.

Does she still not recognize her own lust? Because I could swear I saw a hint of regret yesterday the moment our dirty moment ended. She keeps fighting the attraction, but there's no need. She's mine, and nothing will ever change that, so why not give in?

We both want it. Though, I have to admit, it's mostly because I love the sight of my enemy's daughter groveling at my feet. It gives me a kick to know he had to sacrifice her body and soul in order to keep his business afloat. That the money was worth even her life.

What a wretched fool ... I can't wait to break him by showing him all the footage I've collected of her, and all these filthy little things she does to turn me on. And I can't fucking wait to see the horror settle on his face, and then the defeat that follows naturally.

His life is meaningless to me, and I hope the fucker dies a poor, lonely death.

But first, I have to make her fall for me.

There's no point in flaunting her until she's fully and completely mine by her own volition. It has to be her choice that ruins him, not mine.

I tap my fingers on the table as I take a bite of my cinnamon roll. She's not even touching them or any of the food in front of her, and I wonder why. Did I mess her up that badly? Or is something wrong?

"Aren't you hungry?" I ask, putting down my cinnamon roll. Her eyes follow the rolls as though she wants to take a bite. Why won't she? I know she likes them.

She shakes her head and averts her eyes. "Not after yesterday."

I snort. "C'mon. You can't fool me. You loved what I did, and you know it."

"I don't want to talk about it," she says, picking up her coffee to take a sip.

I narrow my eyes at her. "You don't want to admit it, and that's okay. We'll get there eventually."

"I don't think so," she says. "That's gonna be the day I die."

I laugh and start cutting up my egg on toast. "Should I arrange the funeral then? Because that's going to be any day now."

She throws me a look and picks up an egg, which she eats whole. "Go ahead. I'm slowly dying in this house anyway."

"Now, now, that's a bit of an exaggeration, don't you think?" I muse, taking a bite of my toast. "You're being showered with gifts, plenty of food, and lots of comfort and luxury. What more could you want?"

"My freedom," she says, crossing her arms.

Not this again. We're both on edge but for completely different reasons. For some reason, I can't seem to find my key, and it's been bugging me ever since. I could swear I still had it in my pocket last night, but perhaps I placed it somewhere where even I can't find it.

But I can't show her an inkling of doubt because she'd claw the truth right out of me. And then it'll be a game of catch. I can't let it happen, so I have to remain cool even though she's been anything but cool to me this morning.

If I still can't find my key by noon, I'll call up the locksmith for the extra he keeps in a safety deposit box. If it means I have to interrupt some important business I had to attend, then so be it. I need that goddamn key.

"We've been over this already," I say, taking another bite. "Your freedom is confined to these walls unless I say so."

"But you took me out to that restaurant," she says.

I raise a brow. "So?" What does she want? I know she hated that place, and it was intended to be an intimidation of sorts to both her and her father. I don't know why she'd bring that up again. I thought she'd already moved past it.

"You can take me out again," she says.

Oh … so now she intends to use it against me. Clever girl.

I smile. Perhaps I will someday, but not when she demands it. "I could," I murmur, "but I have lots of work to attend to today."

"What about tomorrow?"

"Tomorrow's busy too, I'm afraid. And the rest of the week," I say, to which her face sours, and for some reason, that hurts my heart. The first time she said she wanted out, I wanted nothing more than to tie her to her bed. I never wanted her to get anywhere close to freedom.

"You're making that up just to keep me here," she hisses. "I can't stay here all the time, Easton. I'm suffocating, can't you see?"

"Hmm …" I mutter.

If I had my way, I'd lock her in a cage and throw away the key. Yet when I look at those beautiful, wistful eyes of hers, I melt away. I can't ignore her desires any longer. I can't get it across my heart to push my own agenda while sacrificing hers. After all, if I don't nurture her, her heart will shrivel away and die.

"How can you expect me to love you when you don't give me anything to love?" she murmurs, the pain in her eyes wounding my soul.

She's right. If I want her fully and completely, I'm going to have to throw her a Hail Mary.

I take a deep breath through my nose, and say, "All right. Since you've behaved well these past few days, I'll let you go out for the day."

Her eyes sparkle with joy.

"If …" I add, holding up my knife, "you let Jill accompany you."

The smile on her face dissipates.

"Take it or leave it," I say, finishing my plate.

"Fine," she snaps as though I'll take the proposition away from her if she doesn't comply. That's a trick I always apply. It works in business … and with women.

I clear my throat. "Jill will take you to do some shopping. She said your closet was empty."

She frowns. "No, I want to decide where we go."

I cock my head and lick my lips for a second.

"Charlotte," I say with a stern voice, "don't push me."

She rubs her lips together and leans back in her chair.

"Do not waste this precious time to nitpick with me. I may be kind, but I am *not* patient," I growl.

"Fine," she says again. "I just want to get out of here."

"To escape me," I say with a grin, after which she looks away. "And I'll allow it. For today."

She doesn't respond anymore, so I continue eating my breakfast, and she does too eventually.

I don't know what's gotten into her. One moment, she's completely into me, almost begging me to kiss her, and then the next moment, she's cold as ice, acting like a complete witch. She switches moods with just a snap of the finger. This girl is certainly a handful. If our children are anything like her, I'll probably have to hire a dozen nannies, for sure.

And to be frank, I can't fucking wait. Because the more time I spend with this woman, the more I realize ... I married the perfect fucking girl for me.

***

Charlotte

As I expected, Easton had the car driven up to the front door, and his driver will drop Jill and me off right in front of the store. I'm sure he did it so he can make sure I won't run off. Jill's not only here to take me shopping but she's also supposed to keep an eye out on me.

That's okay. I didn't think he'd ever let me off the property by myself.

But I didn't expect him to ask Jill to do the stalking.

She's such a friendly person and not at all someone who would keep basement prisoners. Yet she goes along with Easton's wishes, whistling a tune while we're in the car on the way to the store. The eerie sound gives me goose bumps.

"You're not very talkative today, are you?" Jill suddenly asks.

I turn my head toward her, and answer, "Should I be?"

"Well, we're finally going out together," she says with a cheerful smile. "Just you and me!"

I don't know why she's so happy, but it's scary since she knows this is all a farce. I'm still a prisoner inside Easton's mansion. This "going out" isn't really out … just another place where I don't get to walk without supervision. I feel like a kid with a helicopter mom. Although this helicopter mom doesn't know a thing about me, and that could definitely come in handy.

When we arrive at the store, Jill walks to my side and helps me get out, just like Easton always does. He probably told her how to do it because she too locks her arm in mine, preventing me from escaping.

The boutique we walk into is called Luuks, a high-end designer store. Each rack is sorted by color instead of a specific article of clothing, and they're all very minimalistic. Jill sifts through them like crazy, but all I can think about is the notebook clenched between my top and underwear.

I couldn't leave it at his house. The cleaning ladies would probably find it in a heartbeat, no matter where I hid it. There was no safe place in that house, so my only option was to bring it with me.

I hope to God Jill doesn't try to come into the changing room with me.

Or that Easton doesn't open that drawer in his study today.

A sudden hand on my shoulder makes me jolt.

"Oh, I didn't mean to scare you," Jill says.

"No, it's fine. I was just lost in my thoughts," I joke, laughing it off as though it's no big deal.

"Look what I found." She holds up a bunch of dresses and skirts and tops, the type Easton would like. "I even found a cute hairpin to go with it. Pretty, right?"

"Yeah ..." I reply, unsure what she wants from me.

"Let's try them on," she says, and she hurries me to the changing room, grabbing a pair of heels along the way. She hands me the clothes and heels, and says, "If you need help, call out, okay?" And then she closes the curtain.

Finally, I can breathe again. I sit down on the stool and stare at myself in the fancy decorated mirror, wondering what the hell I'm doing here.

I'm in a store. An actual store. In an actual city.

Not his mansion and not his property, but the outside world.

Freedom is right within my grasp. I should reach out and take it, right?

But how? How do I get out of here without Jill noticing, without his bodyguards following me?

And my father … Easton will surely kill him if I'm gone. But maybe there's some way I can prevent it. If I can get to him sooner, I could warn him and tell him to hide. Maybe it could work. But how do I shake off Jill?

And will I be able to survive outside, not knowing any of the people or even the language?

I shiver from the thought and smile at myself in the mirror. Maybe I should just put on this dress and take my mind off things for a second. Maybe being Easton's captive isn't all as bad as it seems.

***

EASTON

With my newly made key in my hand, I immediately go into my study. It's been too long since I last looked at the cameras. I admit I'm addicted to them since she's set foot in my mansion. All I want is to look at her. Is that so wrong?

Well, fuck being right. While she isn't here, I can watch back old footage and enjoy myself. Maybe then I can forget about her not being here. This huge mansion can get lonely pretty fast.

With narrowed eyes, I look around, but nothing seems missing or out of place. Everything is still as I left it the last time I was still here ... when she was in here with me.

Her scent still lingers in the air, and I sniff it up like drugs.

Delicious.

I go to my desk and pull up the laptop, starting the feeds. With my key, I open the drawer to find my lube next to her notebook ... which is no longer here.

My eyes widen as I draw away from my desk and stare at the drawer.

My eyes aren't lying ... the notebook is gone.

What the fuck?!

Who did this? Who took my notebook?

Then it hits me. My disappearing key. Her sudden rage towards me this morning ... and her seduction the night before … it was all a farce.

She stole my key, so she could get into my study and steal the notebook.

Fuck. Fuck!

An unbridled rage flickers the fire inside me, and I roar out loud and reach for my phone.

Time to make a fucking call.

TWENTY-SEVEN

Charlotte

I take off my clothes and put on the long white dress with the slanted shoulders. It looks good on me, and my knees are neatly tucked away underneath the dress, which are always an eye sore. I bunch up my hair and push in the hairpin. When I put on the pumps, the picture is complete. It looks fabulous … but I don't feel the same way. There's a pang of guilt in my stomach, and it shows on my face.

"Yes?" I look up and hold my breath. It's Jill. "Easton? Why are you calling? Is something the matter?"

Shit.

"Oh no, that sounds bad," she continues. "A notebook? No, I haven't seen her carry it."

Double shit.

How does he know the notebook is missing? I still have his key in my panties. There's no way he could've looked inside his drawer unless he has a spare key.

My mind is reeling, and my body is shaking right now.

What do I do now? Easton knows I stole the notebook, and he won't take it lightly. I can't go back to the mansion. But now that Jill's found out too, she'll probably take me back on his orders.

She can't see me, not now. I have to get away.

"Hallo? Heb je hulp nodig?" It's a voice I don't recognize and language I can't speak, so I lift away the curtain a tiny bit. It's the cashier, and she's smiling at me as if she's trying to sell me something and I don't think Jill knows. But maybe I can use this to my advantage.

"Do you speak English?" I ask in a hurry.

"Oh, yes, of course." She clears her throat. "Do you need any help?"

"I love the clothes," I say, sucking up to her. "I just … I was wondering if I could use your bathroom?" I add a cutesy smile as a gesture of goodwill.

She frowns and parts her lips, then rubs them together as though she's contemplating it. "I'm sorry, but it's for staff only—"

"It's just that I'm pregnant, and I have this terrible urge every time I leave the house, even if just to shop. Maybe I should've stayed home."

I'm making it up as I go along, but her eyes light up the moment I mention that I shouldn't have come here.

"Oh, congratulations! Hmm ... I'm sure we could make an exception for you," she says with a wink.

Of course, she suddenly can. No one likes to lose a customer, especially not when they're loaded with cash, which I'm sure she knows, judging from the way she's staring at my diamond ring.

"That'd be amazing. Thank you," I answer, and I push the curtain farther back.

"C'mon, it's in the back," she says, walking off through the store.

Before I follow her, I check to see if Jill's around, but she's still staring at the clothing racks, comparing two different sizes of the same dress.

I tag along behind the cashier, who's walking as though she has a plug up her ass. But her slow walk through the door in the back causes me to catch a glimpse of something important. A key dangling out of her pocket. A key that might open the escape door right in front of us.

She swiftly spins on her heels as we reach the bathroom door. "There you go."

She holds the door open for me as if she's waiting for me to go inside so she can lock it behind me, but I know that's not how these toilet doors work. I'm just paranoid.

So paranoid ... that I bump into her on the way inside.

"Sorry!" I mutter as she catches me. "Sorry. The

pregnancy's made me all woozy." I laugh, and she laughs too. Then I go inside and lock the door behind me.

But I don't pee.

I sit there in complete darkness ... staring at the key in my hand.

She didn't even notice that I took it when I bumped into her because she was too busy trying to keep me from falling. I can't believe this sly trick worked.

My heart pounds, and beads of sweat trickle down my back as I wait a few seconds until I hear nothing but my own breaths. Then I unlock the door and go out. Jill's voice from the front of the store is audible right through the door.

"Charlotte? Where is the girl with the pink hair? Uh ... War iz Charlotte? Rosé har?" She's trying to speak Dutch and failing miserably, but she sounds more agitated by the second. I don't have any time to lose, so I don't think twice before I turn the other way toward the fire exit with the large green "escape" button on it. The irony isn't wasted on me as I slip the key into the lock and open the door.

I burst out into the sunlight, blinking a couple of times so my eyes can adjust to the brightness. I breathe in a couple of times, cherishing the smell of freedom ...

And I come face to face with one of Easton's guards.

Shit.

He was probably keeping the coast clear here, in case I'd try to escape.

I can't even blink before he grabs me and holds me tight.

I squeal, but he covers my mouth, so I stomp on his foot. His grip on my body loosens for a second, and I spin on my heels to make a run for it. He catches up within three steps and jumps on me from behind. We tumble to the floor, and I claw at his face, scratching his cheeks.

He twists me around on the ground and grabs me with his burly arms, throwing me over his shoulder. My heart races, and my mind is reeling.

No. I can't go back. I can't ever go back.

In desperation, I grab the hairpin in my hair … and stick it right into his side multiple times.

The bodyguard collapses to his knees, and I fall right on top of him.

I scramble to my feet and glance at him over my shoulder. My feet are ready to go, but I can't leave him like that, can I?

Blood pours from his wounds as he growls in pain, and guilt rushes through my veins. But I can't tend to him. I won't get another chance to escape, I have to grasp this moment. I have to go … *now*!

"I'm sorry," I mutter, and I turn and run off.

"Charlotte, no!"

A sharp voice makes me turn my head.

It's Jill, her eyes widened, her jaw dropped as we come face to face while she clenches the doorpost, and I'm outside in the alley. The moment of silence seems eternal. Her eyes reflect the pain of betrayal, the regret of not stopping me, and all the consequences she'll have to endure because of my escape.

I'm sorry for putting all of this on her because I know Easton won't treat her well once he finds out, but I can't stop now that I've come so far.

I wish I could say goodbye. That I could tell her I didn't hate her, I don't blame her for what happened to me, and I wish she'd make a better choice the next time around.

After all, Easton will still be the same power-hungry control freak.

But one thing's for sure … it's not going to be me.

And with a final smile sent her way, I drop her pager on the ground and run.

THANK YOU FOR READING!

Thank you so much for reading A Debt Owed. If you want to know when the next book goes live, sign up for my newsletter here: www.bit.ly/clarissanewsletter

You can also stay up to date via my website: www.clarissawild.com

I'd love to talk to you! You can find me on Facebook: www.facebook.com/ClarissaWildAuthor, make sure to click LIKE.

You can also join the Fan Club: www.facebook.com/groups/FanClubClarissaWild and talk with other readers!

Enjoyed this book? You could really help out by leaving a review on Amazon and Goodreads. Thank you!

ALSO BY CLARISSA WILD

Dark Romance

Savage Men Series
Delirious Series
Indecent Games Series
Killer & Stalker
Mr. X
Twenty-One
Ultimate Sin
VIKTOR
FATHER

New Adult Romance

Fierce Series
Blissful Series
Ruin

Erotic Romance

The Billionaire's Bet Series
Enflamed Series
Unprofessional Bad Boys Series

Visit Clarissa Wild's website for current titles.
https://www.clarissawild.com

ABOUT THE AUTHOR

Clarissa Wild is a New York Times & USA Today Bestselling author of Dark Romance and Contemporary Romance novels. She is an avid reader and writer of swoony stories about dangerous men and feisty women. Her other loves include her hilarious husband, her cutie pie son, her two crazy but cute dogs, and her ninja cat that sometimes thinks he's a dog too. In her free time, she enjoys watching all sorts of movies, playing video games, reading tons of books, and cooking her favorite meals.

Want to be informed of new releases and special offers? Sign up for Clarissa Wild's newsletter on her website www.clarissawild.com.

Visit Clarissa Wild on Amazon for current titles.

Printed in Poland
by Amazon Fulfillment
Poland Sp. z o.o., Wrocław